Bedtime Me Stories for Kids

A Collection of Short Tales with Positive Affirmations to Help Children and Toddlers Fall Asleep Fast in Bed and Have a Relaxing Night's Sleep with Beautiful Dreams

Mindfulness Fairy and Daisy Relaxing

No warranties of any kind are declared or implied. Readers acknowledge that the author is not engaging in the rendering of legal, financial, medical or professional advice.

The content within this book has been derived from various sources. Please consult a licensed professional before attempting any techniques outlined in this book.

By reading this document, the reader agrees that under no circumstances is the author responsible for any losses, direct or indirect, which are incurred as a result of the use of the information contained within this document, including, but not limited to, — errors, omissions, or inaccuracies.

Table of Contents

Contents

Introduction

Welcome to *Bedtime Meditation Short Stories for Kids.*

In this whimsical book, you will find many wonderful stories to help you fall asleep each night. Plus, you will explore wonderful new skills that you can use to help you learn how to relax your body so you can have a comfortable, sound sleep all night long.

Before we get started with stories, I want to talk to you about important bedtime routines.

Do you have a bedtime routine?

A bedtime routine is something you do every single night to help you get ready for bed so that when you crawl into bed each night, you know that you are ready for a sound sleep.

Having a proper bedtime routine helps you make sure that when you crawl into bed every night, you are not going to find yourself feeling distracted by your thoughts.

This way, you know that you are completely ready for bed, so you can just relax, listen to your story, and fall asleep.

Everybody's bedtime routine is different, but you should always make sure to include brushing your teeth, combing your hair, and putting on a comfortable pair of pajamas.

You can also have a sip of water, make sure your bed is cozy for you to get into, and grab your favorite stuffed animal so that you have someone comfy and warm to sleep next to.

Don't forget to say goodnight to your family, too!

Once you have finished your bedtime routine, and you are sure that you are ready to fall asleep, you can pick your bedtime story and start relaxing.

Make sure you listen to each story and follow along, as each one has a relaxing meditation for you to follow to help you get nice and comfortable for a good night's rest.

This is important, as it will help you wake up refreshed and ready for each new day!

Are you ready to get started with your bedtime meditation? Choose your story to begin!

Chapter 1: Lavender Chases A Butterfly

Tonight, we are going to enjoy a wonderful story about a small purple fairy named Lavender!

Before we do, though, we need to make sure that you are nice and comfortable and ready for a great night's sleep.

So, to get started, I want you to make sure that you are tucked in comfortably and that you are ready to lay still and focus on your breathing.

Make sure that your blankets are just warm enough, and that if you cuddle a stuffed animal to sleep that your stuffy is tucked in close to you, too.

Now, I want you to focus on your nose.
Take a moment to notice the air going in and out of your nose.

Can you feel each breath you take? Feel how that air feels as it goes in your nose when you breathe in and out your nose when you breathe back out.

Breathing is something we do not usually think about because our body does it automatically.

Sometimes, thinking about a simple breath can help you relax and feel more comfortable at the moment.

As you keep focusing on the breath in your nose, I want you to follow that breath the next time you inhale.

Where does that breath go?
Do you feel your chest and tummy expanding when you breathe in?

This is your lungs inflating with each breath, giving your body plenty of room for air to come in and nourish your body with oxygen.

When you breathe out, can you follow that breath all the way back out?

Feel your chest and tummy falling down as the air comes back out, and you blow it out into your room.

Now, I am going to count out each breath, and I want you to follow each breath that I count out.

Starting with one, follow your breath all the way through your nose and into your lungs, and two follow your breath all the way out of your lungs and out of your nose and back into the room.

Now three, follow another breath back through your nose and into your lungs, and four follow that breath all the way back out through your nose and into the room.

Five, following your breath in, and six, following your breath out.

Again, seven, follow your breath into your lungs, and eight follow your breath all the way out through your nose.

One more time: nine follow your breath in through your nose and into your lungs, and then follow your breath out of your lungs and out of your nose.

Now, I want you to focus on letting your breath be natural.

Do not try to control it, but instead let your body natural control your breath and help you breathe in and out on its own, just like it does every single day when you are playing, spending time with your family, or studying.

As you continue to relax into your breath, I want to tell you about a fairy named Lavender.

Lavender is a beautiful small fairy, no taller than your thumb.

She has light purple hair, a small green shirt made of a leaf that her mom made for her, and a purple skirt made of orchids.

Lavender lives in the Mystery Forest with her sisters Sage, Berry, and Blossom.

Her favorite thing to do every day is playing with her sisters in the forest.

There, they like to play tag, hide and go seek, and soccer with a small blueberry that they use for a soccer ball.

Unlike her sisters, Lavender also really liked to play by herself.

Sometimes, while her sisters could be found playing hide and go seek, Lavender would be sitting somewhere by herself, painting the scenery using the juice from berries as her paint.

Whenever she painted, Lavender always noticed how the Mystery Forest was so peaceful.

As she painted, she would see frogs relaxing on lily pads, dragonflies dancing in the sunlight, and bees massaging the pollen out of flowers that scattered the forest floor.

Lavender would always try to paint these creatures enjoying the calmness of the afternoon, but sometimes they would move on before she could finish her painting. Still, she tried anyway.

One day, while her sisters were playing tag, Lavender decided to hang out by the Mysterious Creek and paint a frog that was relaxing on a lily pad.

As she got all of her paints ready, she noticed an unusual butterfly perched on a rock.

This butterfly was unlike anything she had ever seen before, and it caught Lavender's attention immediately.

Unlike the other butterflies she had seen, Lavender noticed that this particular butterfly was incredibly colorful.

It had light purple sparkly wings, just like Lavender's hair.

The butterfly also had pink, orange, green, and blue speckles all over it.

Lavender was amused by the uniqueness of this butterfly and decided that she would paint the butterfly instead of the frog.

As soon as Lavender began to turn her easel around so she could see the butterfly better, it took off.

"Wait!" Lavender shouted, chasing the butterfly.

She really wanted to paint it, so she chased it down, hoping she could encourage it to land again long enough for her to paint it.

"Wait!" she shouted again, running across the side of the creek.

She hopped over rocks, moss, and twigs as she reached her hands up in the air and chased the butterfly.

The butterfly continued flying away, swirling and changing directions every few seconds.

Determined to catch the butterfly, Lavender kept running.

As the butterfly flew away faster, Lavender ran faster.

She ran so fast that she tripped over a small root sticking out next to the creek, but that didn't stop her.

Lavender jumped back to her feet and, without brushing the dirt off, kept running.

Her wings tried hard to flutter and lift her up into the air so she could chase the butterfly even better, but Lavender and her sisters were still too small for their wings to work.

According to her mom, there would be at least another three moon cycles before her wings were strong enough to carry her.

As the butterfly dodged Lavender's hands and dipped and curled along the creek side, Lavender ran faster.

Eventually, the butterfly flew over to the other side of the creek.

Not thinking about what she was doing, Lavender hopped onto some scattered rocks over the creek and tried to jump to the other side.

Before she could stop herself, she jumped so far she barely landed on a rock, and she realized there were no more rocks for her to jump on.

Looking back at where she came from, she realized she was too far to jump back.

Although the creek may have been moving slowly to a human like you or me, this creek was very deep and fast for such a small fairy like Lavender.

Scared, she sat down and held her knees into her chest.

As she looked around, Lavender realized she had run much further than she thought, and she had no idea how to get back home.

Realizing it was no longer being chased, the butterfly landed on a nearby branch and seemed to watch over Lavender as she sat there on the rock in the water.

"What will I ever do now?"

Lavender cried, scared that she might never see her family again.

The butterfly sat patiently, gently flapping its wings and relaxing in the sunlight.

Before long, the sunlight slowly started to disappear as the sun began to set for the evening.

Now, Lavender was really getting scared because she realized she had never been out in the Mystery Forest by herself at night before.

Her parents warned her of all of the dangerous creatures that might be hiding in the forest and told her and her sisters to always come back home at sunset so that they could stay safe and warm.

"What if they don't find me?" Lavender whimpered.

The butterfly continued to remain perched nearby as if it were staying close to Lavender to keep her safe as the forest grew darker around them.

Suddenly, Lavender could hear her name being called in the distance.

"Lavender?" she heard.

"Yes, I'm over here!" she jumped up to her feet, waving and looking toward where the voice was coming from.

"Lavender!" her Dad said excitedly, flying over to the rock and scooping her up into his arms.

"What are you doing all the way out here?" he asked.

Lavender frowned and looked down toward the water.

"Well, I was painting out by the creek, and there was this *really beautiful butterfly!* I really wanted to paint it, but then it started flying away, so I chased it! Before I knew it, I was stuck all the way out here on this rock, and I couldn't get home. I'm sorry Dad."

She said, hiding her face in his shoulder.

Lavender's Dad just chuckled and said, "It's okay, Lavender, mistakes happen. I found you, and you are safe, and that's all that matters. That must have been one butterfly!" He smiled.

"Yeah! It is! It's right over there!" Lavender said, pointing to where the butterfly had been.

As she did, she realized the butterfly had already disappeared.

"It was just there!" Lavender said, confused.

"I know, sweetie." Her Dad said.

"Let's get you back home, your mom is worried about you, and she has some delicious berry soup ready for us when we get back."

"Berry soup? That's my favorite!" Lavender smiled, hugging her dad's neck.

Her dad flew them both all the way back home, where they enjoyed berry soup with her family.

When they were done, Lavender went to sleep.

The next morning, Lavender woke up and immediately took out all of her painting supplies.

She sat outside all morning, closing her eyes and then painting a little here and a little there.

When she was done, she had completely painted the butterfly that she had seen the day before!

Then, she showed it to her parents.

"Wow, that really is a beautiful butterfly!" her dad smiled, looking at her painting.

"It sure was." Lavender smiled, wishing she would see the butterfly once again. Just as she made the wish, the butterfly flew by her house again, toward the creek.

"See, there it is!" Lavender pointed, excitedly jumping up and down!

"Wow!" her sisters said, staring in wonder. "That is one beautiful butterfly."

Her mother smiled.

"I know," Lavender said, giggling.

Later that afternoon, Lavender's dad came to talk to her.

"Lavender?" he asked.

"Yeah, dad?"

"I wanted to let you know that I am so proud of you for chasing your dreams of painting that beautiful butterfly you saw." he smiled.

"Thanks, dad."

"Next time you want to chase your dreams, make sure you ask for help.

Sometimes, your dreams are so big that you might not know how to achieve them on your own.

You might even find yourself in danger like you were yesterday when you were lost at the creek.

But if you ask for help from someone like your mom or me, then you can chase your dreams and be safe, too.

Sometimes, you never know who might have the answer to help you get there." he said, hugging Lavender close.

"Okay, dad, the next time I am going to chase my dreams, I will come ask you or mom for help, first." she smiled.

"Great honey, now I want you to come look at this." her dad said, holding her hand and bringing her back toward the house.

As they got closer, Lavender saw her mom holding out a special piece of fruit.

"What is that?" Lavender asked.

"This is a gem fruit." Lavender's mom smiled, holding it up into the air.

"A gem fruit?" Lavender asked.

"Yes, it is a very rare form of fruit that is known for attracting gem butterflies, just like the one you saw?"

"Gem butterflies?" Lavender's eyes widened, "you mean you have seen these butterflies before?" she excitedly asked.

"Yes! I have been growing these fruits behind our house for the past month, hoping to attract some of these beautiful butterflies. I see it has worked." she smiled.

Just then, several gem butterflies just like the one Lavender painted, came flying toward her mom.

"See?" she smiled. "Here, take this fruit," she said, passing the gem fruit to Lavender.

Lavender held it, and just like that, a butterfly landed next to her and started eating some of the fruit she was holding.

Lavender giggled, "it tickles!" she said, giving the fruit to the butterfly.

Lavender, her sisters, and their parents spent the afternoon giggling and feeding the gem butterflies.

As they did, Lavender smiled, knowing that she fulfilled her dream of painting the special butterfly and that now she would get to see these special beautiful butterflies even more because her mom was growing a special fruit to feed them.

I love telling the story of Lavender because she always reminds me to chase my dreams.

Sometimes, chasing our dreams can be scary, but when we have the loving support of our family, we can do anything.

Make sure that when you do chase your dreams, though, that your parents always know where you are going and what you are doing so that you do not get lost as Lavender did in the creek!

So, what do you dream of in your life?

As you do dream for it, you can help yourself reach those dreams even better by repeating these positive affirmations to yourself:

"I am great at chasing my dreams."

"My dreams are perfectly suited to me."

"I will always chase my dreams."

"I know that I am supported in chasing my dreams."

"I love my big dreams for my life."

"I can ask for help when I need it."

"My dream for my life is so fun!"

"I am a great dreamer."

"I can dream as many dreams as I want to."

"I will always achieve my dreams if I keep trying.

Chapter 2: Rex Has a Great Day

Tonight we are going to talk about my good friend Rex and his great day.

Before we can talk about Rex and his great day, though, I want to make sure that you are super comfortable and relaxed so that you can enjoy this story as much as I will!

Are you ready? Let's get started!

Make sure that you have done your entire bedtime routine, that you are comfortably tucked in under the covers, and that you have your stuffy to sleep with if you use one.

As you get cozy, I want you to lay on your back and lay your arms down by your side.

Keep your legs nice and straight, as if you are trying to be as tall as you can be when you lay in your bed.

Tonight we are going to practice a skill called muscle relaxation.

To practice muscle relaxation, all you have to do is listen to the part of your body.

I tell you to relax, and then let that part of your body completely relax.

Do you think that you can do that? Great!

Start by letting your feet relax completely.

Then, let your legs all the way through your shins, knees, and thighs relax completely.

Now, relax your bum and your hips.

Next, relax your lower tummy and your lower back.

As you relax each part of your body, feel it growing extremely comfortable and ready for a long night's sleep.

Now, let that relaxation feeling move up into the middle of your tummy and the middle of your back.

Next, it moves up into your chest and your upper back.

Feel the feeling of relaxation moving through your shoulders, then down through your arms.

Notice your arms relaxing down through your elbows, wrists, and all the way to the tips of your fingers and thumbs.

Now, let your neck relax completely.

Then, let your head relax completely.

By now, you should be feeling much calmer and relaxed and ready to listen to a great bedtime story.

My friend Rex is a really nice guy.

He is a little bit taller than I am, with brown hair and brown eyes.

Usually, he wears a simple white t-shirt and a pair of dark blue shorts when we play together.

I always thought it was cool that his mom lets him wear white because my mom always says I get my white clothes too dirty when I play in them, so she makes me wear different colors like green, orange, or brown.

The other day after dinner, I went over to Rex's house and asked him how he was doing.

He told me that he had a really great day.

"Really? Why?" I asked him. And so he told me.

Rex's day started out early when birds were chirping outside of his window.

He woke up to peek out the window, and he saw a blue bird feeding a worm to her baby birds!

He said it was the coolest thing he had ever seen as he watched these babies eat the worm from their mom.

As he was watching, his own mom came into his room to let him know it was time to get up, but he was already up!

She was so surprised that he woke up before his alarm that she sat with him, and they watched the birds together for a while.

When the birds were ready to fall asleep, Rex and his mom decided to go to the kitchen and start making their own breakfast.

Because of their morning spent watching the birds eating, Rex's mom decided to make eggs in a nest!

He told me that it means that his mom cut a hole out of a piece of toast and cooked an egg in it so that it looked like his egg was in a nest just like the baby birds.

She also made bacon for their breakfast, and they pretended the bacon was worms as they dipped it into the warm runny yolks of their eggs.

After breakfast was done, Rex poured himself a big fresh cup of orange juice and enjoyed every last sip of it.

Then, it was time to get ready for the day.

Today was a Saturday, so Rex did not have any school.

It was also a special day because his dad had taken his brother to a soccer game, so he and his mom were enjoying some quiet time together, which is something he enjoyed doing.

He told me about how he went and brushed his teeth, combed his hair, washed his face, and put on his fresh clothes out of the dryer.

They were so warm that they made him feel even comfier!

After he was dressed, Rex's mom told him that she had a really special surprise for him.

So, they put on their shoes and went to the car so that she could drive them to the surprise.

As they were driving, Rex and his mom shared many funny jokes about birds and other animals that made him laugh the whole way.

Then, they arrived at his grandma's house.

When they got inside, his grandma smiled and welcomed him in and asked him to take off his shoes and put on some boots instead!

"Why? It's sunny outside!" he asked, slipping on a pair of rubber boots.

"You'll see." his grandma smiled.

Rex followed his grandma to the backyard, and when they got there, Rex saw all of his cousins wearing rubber boots and splashing in a mud puddle that his grandpa was making in the garden with the hose.

Rex laughed and ran out to the garden to splash around with his cousins while his mom and aunties and uncles enjoyed a drink of lemonade with his grandma and grandpa.

When they were all done splashing, Rex joined his mom for some lemonade.

While he sat there, drinking the lemonade, his dad and brother came out!

The soccer game was over, and so Rex got to play in the mud puddles again with his brother, too.

Rex loves playing with his brother.

Once they were done, Rex and his brother and all of their cousins cleaned up and went inside to enjoy a delicious supper together.

They feasted on ham, potatoes, salad, carrots, stuffing, squash, spaghetti, and broccoli with cheese sauce.

When they were done, they enjoyed a delicious cake that his grandma had prepared for them.

At the end of the dinner, each of the children went and cleaned themselves up, and the parents helped clean up the kitchen.

Then, Rex and his brother and his father and mother got ready, said goodbye to their grandma and grandpa, and left to go back home.

On their way home, Rex's dad mentioned that he had run into Rex's teacher at his brother's soccer game.

While his dad and his teacher were talking, his teacher told his dad that Rex had been one of the only students in the whole classroom to get an A on the homework assignment that was being graded that weekend.

Rex felt really proud, and his brother even gave him a high five!

When they got home, Rex went inside and took off his shoes, then went back to his bedroom to see if he could see the nest with the baby birds again.

Outside of his window, a mommy bird, daddy bird, and four baby birds were all nestled together inside of their nest sleeping.

"I wonder if they're dreaming about worms?" he asked, laughing.

"Maybe." his mom smiled.

Then, his brother went to work on his homework, his dad went to read the newspaper, and his mom went to read a book.

That's when I came over.

I was so happy to listen to Rex's great day that I almost forgot about my own day when he asked!

While Rex enjoyed all of that time playing with his family, I had spent the afternoon watching movies with my own family.

Although we had two entirely different days, we both had really great days.

We high fived and then went on to hang out, enjoying a great night together.

We played board games, watched movies, and even enjoyed a glass of chocolate milk that his mom gave us!

Then, when it got late, I went home and went to bed while Rex and his family went to sleep, too.

It was a really great day for both of us, and I was so happy to celebrate having a wonderful day with my good friend Rex.

I love times like this where I get to remember how fun it is to celebrate my friends' wins and celebrate my own wins, too.

In life, it is important to remember that if you care about someone, you should celebrate their happiness and success with them, too.

That is why I was so happy to celebrate Rex today, and he was happy to celebrate with me, too!

What are you celebrating right now?

Are you going to wake up in the morning and have a really great day?

I bet you will, too!

Here are some great affirmations to help you remember to have a really great day, and to celebrate the people around you that you love when they have a great day, too.

"I feel happy and successful today."
"I have everything I need to have a great day."
"I am going to have a great day today."
"I am able to make decisions that help me have a great day."
"I am happy about my great day."
"I am great at having a great time."
"I listen to my parents so that we can all have a great day."
"I celebrate my loved ones having a great day."
"I make great decisions for myself."
"I have everything I need to be happy."

Chapter 3: Sally Plays Imagination

Playing with your imagination is so fun.

Do you like to play with your imagination, too?

Our imaginations can take us anywhere we want if we just ask it to.

With our imaginations, we can picture ourselves in a sailboat sailing the ocean, overlooking the city from a tall castle, or even running in a field with farm animals.

We can do anything we want with our imaginations if we are willing to.

Tonight, we are going to talk about Sally and the experience she had playing with her imagination.

Sally went to many incredible places with her imagination and had a really fun time enjoying each of these places.

The best part is: she never even left her bedroom to go there!

Before we can explore Sally's imagination with her, though, we need to make sure that you are good and comfortable and ready for bed.

Make sure that you do your bedtime routine, get a sip of water, and get yourself really comfy in bed so that you are ready for the story of Sally and her imagination.

Tonight, to help you get all the way relaxed, we are going to do an easy breathing meditation that will help you calm your entire body down so that you can have a really great sleep.

Are you ready? Let's begin.

To start your breathing meditation tonight, I want you to put one hand on your tummy.

As you lay there, I want you to breathe in and push your hand toward the sky with your tummy, using only your breath.

Now, breathe out and feel your hand fall all the way down toward your bed as your tummy falls down.

Again, breathe in and push your hand toward the sky with your tummy, then breathe out and let your hand fall all the way back toward the bed.

I am going to count, and with each count, I want you to breathe in, and then on the next count breathe out.

Just like this: one, breathe in and push your hand toward the sky, two, breathe out and drop your hand toward the bed.

Three, breathe in and push your hand toward the sky, and four, let your hand fall toward your bed as you breathe out.

Five, breathe in, six, breathe out.

Seven, breathe in, eight, breathe out.

And one more time, nine, breathe in and push your hand toward the sky, and breathe out and let your hand fall back toward the bed.

Now I want you to lay your hand down by your side and let yourself breathe naturally.

This natural breathing rhythm will be just like the one you do all day every day when you don't even realize you are breathing!

Your body just does it naturally for you, and that is exactly what it will do all night long.

Now that you are relaxed, I want you to bring your focus to my words, and I am going to tell you a great story about how Sally used her imagination to take a big vacation without ever even leaving her bedroom.

Sally has a really strong imagination, and I bet you do, too!

Sally's day playing with her imagination started out with her being bored in her bedroom all by herself.

Her mom was busy baking, and her dad was busy mowing the lawn, and Sally's sister was over at her friend's house.

Sally was all by herself in her bedroom feeling sorry for herself when suddenly she was inspired to start playing with her toys and having fun with her imagination.

First, Sally imagined that her small pillow her grandma had made her was a blue dragon.

She flew the blue dragon all around her bedroom, pretending it was chasing away intruders from her castle.

As the blue dragon continued to fly around her room, her dolls and farm animals all scurried away to their homes, trying to hide from the dragon.

"Roar!" she shouted, chasing the animals and dolls as they all made their way to their homes to hide away from her.

Outside of the dollhouse, a purple llama got confused.

It could not decide whether to go to the barn for the farm animals or into the house for the dolls.

The barn for the farm animals was already full of pigs, cows, sheep, chickens, and goats.

"But animals aren't allowed in the house!" the purple llama said, still trying to decide.

"Roar!" the dragon circled around the roofs of the buildings, getting ready to torch anyone who was not yet hiding away safely inside.

Right before the dragon blew his firey breath, the purple llama ran into the house with the dolls and hid in the kitchen.

Soon, the dragon grew bored and stopped circling the houses.

He laid down on Sally's bed and watched over the land, making sure that everyone stayed inside so that he would not have to start flying around and chasing them into their houses again.

As everything settled down, Sally's dolls began playing inside of their home.

One of Sally's dolls decided to go to the kitchen to make food for everyone, just like Sally's mom was doing for her own family.

When she got into the kitchen, the doll screamed.

"What is a purple llama doing in the kitchen?!" she said, running out.

One by one, all of the dolls came in to see the purple llama in the kitchen.

"Shoo!" one of the dolls started saying, pushing the purple llama out of the house.

"Is that someone outside I see?" the blue dragon shouted, getting ready to start flying around again.

Scared for the safety of the purple llama, one of Sally's dolls ran out of the house and started protecting the purple llama.

"No, nothing to see here!" Sally said, covering the doll and the purple llama.
Just like that, Sally, her doll, and the purple llama took off on an adventure.

As the blue dragon started chasing them, they took off to hide in the woods.

First, they hid under the trees, but the dragon torched all the trees!

So, they started running for the water because Sally knew that water stopped the fire from spreading.

"The dragon won't be able to torch us here!" she said, hiding herself, her doll, and the purple llama in the creek under the forest.

The dragon torched the trees surrounding the creek, and while they never caught on fire, the water got *really* hot!

"Let's go!" Sally said, grabbing her doll and purple llama and taking off running.

They ran down the creek, through the field next to the farmer's house, and back toward the barn and the dollhouse.

"You can't bring them in here!" the other dolls said, keeping the door closed from Sally, the other doll, and the purple llama.

"Fine!" Sally said, picking them up and running once again.

This time, they ran through a city, across the roads (after looking both ways, of course) and down under a playground that they saw next to a tall school building.

"Surely, the dragon won't find us here!" Sally said as they looked back at all of the stuff the dragon had torched.

"Are you sure?" the purple llama asked, hiding deeper in Sally's pocket.
"I'm sure!" Sally smiled, tapping her pocket to comfort the purple llama.

As they continued to hide, Sally heard her mom calling her for dinner.

Still, she stayed quiet: she did not want to let the dragon know where they are, after all, as the dragon might burn her friends while she ate dinner!

Sally heard her mom calling again, and this time she pressed even deeper into her hiding spot, scared that her mom would let the dragon know where they were.

Finally, her mom called one more time, and this time, the dragon spun around and started chasing her mom!

"Mom, look out!" Sally said, running to her mom.

"What's that?" her mom asked, scooping Sally up in her arms.

"The dragon was coming to get us, and you saved us!" Sally smiled, looking down at the blue dragon perched on the side of her bed, which was looking out over the dollhouse and the barn full of animals.

Sally patted her pocket and then pulled out her doll and purple llama and showed them to her mom,

"See? You saved us."

She smiled, snuggling into her mom's shoulder.

Sally's mom just laughed and said, "my, what a creative girl you are!" as she hugged Sally even closer.

"I know." Sally smiled.
Having an imagination is a great way to play.

When you have a good imagination, you can go anywhere you want, and no one can even stop you!

You can play with blue dragons or orange dragons, purple llamas, or pink sheep; you can travel to the city, the woods, or the river.

You can do anything you want when you have an imagination, and you never even have to go too far to play with it.

Cool, right?

Do you play with your imagination often?

Strengthening your imagination can help you have even more fun when you play, too.

The world can be anything you want it to be if your imagination is strong enough to help you get there.

Tonight, let's enjoy some helpful affirmations that will help you have even more fun with your imagination.

This way, you can build your own creativity and have just as much fun as Sally did with her blue dragon!

The positive affirmations you can use to help you have even more creativity in your life are:

"I am a creative person."

"My imagination is so strong."

"I always have new ideas."

"Playing with my creativity is fun."

"Playing with my imagination is fun."

"I can create anything my heart desires."

"My talents are unique to me."

"I always take time to do creative things every day."

"I have a vast imagination."

"Creative energy flows through me."

Chapter 4: Gilbert's Day of Fun

Learning how to have fun no matter what is going on is a useful skill that everyone can develop.

When you know how to have fun, then it does not matter what you are doing, you can find a way to make it a fun experience.

One of my good friends, Gilbert, taught me a great lesson in fun when he chose to have fun even though things were not going his way.

Tonight, we are going to talk about Gilbert and his experience of having fun even when things do not go your way.

To help you get comfortable so that you can listen to Gilbert's story, we are going to do a muscle relaxation technique that will help you relax.

This simple skill is going to help you learn how to bring calm to your body even when you are feeling restless or too awake to relax.

To do this skill, all you have to do is listen to my voice, and I will tell you what part of your body to relax, and when.

We are going to start this muscle relaxation with your toes.

I want you to feel your toes relaxing completely.

If you can, visualize a golden light coming into your toes and helping them relax so that they can have a comfortable sleep all night long.

See this golden light and relaxing energy moving into the bottom of your feet now, covering it completely and then wrapping around the top of your feet.

Then, see this relaxing energy wrap through your ankles.

As the golden light continues to climb, feel the bottoms of your legs starting to relax, as that relaxing feeling moves all the way up to your knees.

Then, feel it move past your knees and into your thighs, all the way toward your hips.

Feel all of the muscles between your knees and hips relaxing completely as this golden light swirls through them and helps them feel completely at peace.

Now, see this golden light moving into your lower tummy and back.

Feel the muscles in your lower tummy and back relax, as the light starts to move up into the middle of your tummy and the middle of your back.

Let yourself continue to relax even deeper as this relaxing feeling and golden light moves into your chest and your upper back, and then wraps around your shoulders like a vest.

Feel that relaxing energy moving down your arms, toward your elbows, then through to your wrists and through your palms and fingers, all the way down to your fingertips.

Next, let that relaxing light and feeling move through your neck, the back of your head, and up over just like a hood on your jacket.

Feel the relaxation moving down into your forehead and toward your nose, lips, and chin.

Now, feel your entire body feeling completely relaxed as you notice that each part of your body is now ready for a great night's sleep.

If you are ready now, we will start talking about Gilbert and his important lesson about how he continued to have fun even though things were not going his way.

This is an important lesson to learn because sometimes things will not always go your way, but you will still have to choose how to react to those situations, even if it feels very hard to do so.

Gilbert plays on a soccer team with all of his friends.

Each Saturday morning, they play together in a game against other teams.

They practice for those games all week long after school, where they learn how to kick the ball, score goals, and protect their net from having goals scored against them.

Each player on the team was being coached to do the best they could do, and they felt confident that they were getting better.

Still, when the time came for the games to be played on Saturday, Gilbert's team always lost.

For some reason, even when they felt that they knew what they were doing, they would get shy around other teams, and it would cause them to play differently.

Gilbert would fumble over the ball and trip on the field, and his friends would do the same.

Their goalie would have a harder time noticing the ball coming toward them and would struggle to get in front of it so it would not get into their net.

All of them had a really difficult time playing under the pressure of an audience and with a different team around, and so they always lost the game.

Gilbert's team mates would often get upset with themselves and each other for not playing better and not winning the game.

They would point fingers, blame each other, and get angry whenever they lost.

One time, one of his teammates even threw the ball at another player on a different and tried to start a fight with them because the team they had lost to was being rude about their win.

Gilbert's coach and the other team's coach stopped the fight so that no one got hurt, and the two teams went their own ways.

Even though Gilbert's team members would get so angry and upset that they lost, Gilbert never felt the same way.

Instead of being angry with himself or his team for losing, he felt compassion for them.

Gilbert knew that they were all feeling shy and scared under pressure and so it made playing harder for them.

Rather than getting angry with his teammates, he always celebrated them and encouraged them to try harder next time.

In practice, he would always high five his teammates when they were doing good, and on the field, during games, he would still cheer them on even if they were losing.

Gilbert thought that it was important that his teammates knew that no matter how they scored, they were still great soccer players.

One Saturday, in particular, Gilbert's team got really upset that they lost the game.

They had been losing games all season, and they were starting to feel really defeated.

Some of them even wanted to quit because they felt like they were never going to be good enough to have any success on the soccer field.

Gilbert felt sad that his own teammates wanted to quit the game because he had so much fun playing with all of them each week and on Saturdays.

Gilbert felt like his teammates had become good friends of his, and he did not want to see his friends giving up on something they enjoyed just because they felt like they were always losing or there was no point in playing anymore.

On his way home from that game, Gilbert talked to his dad.

"Everyone wants to quit soccer because we are not winning, but I do not want to lose my friends. I have fun playing with them every week!" Gilbert said, sadly.

"Maybe your friends need help learning about sportsmanship and about how to have fun no matter how you score in the game." Gilbert's dad suggested.

"I don't think they will listen to me, I always cheer them on, but they never seem to care!

Even though we have good friendships, they still get angry and want to quit even when I am a good sport. What can I do, dad?" Gilbert asked.

"Maybe next time you are in the field, you can talk to your friends about sportsmanship.

You are very good at sportsmanship, and maybe they will be willing to learn from you." Gilbert's dad smiled, patting Gilbert's hand.

"Okay, dad, I will try that."

At their next practice, the team was different.

Everyone showed up, but no one was trying as hard as they usually did.

Balls were flying all over the place, everyone was grumpy, and some kids were just sitting on the sidelines as if they had given up completely.

Gilbert walked up to a few of his teammates who were sitting down and asked, "why don't you come play with us?"

"What's the point? We will just lose this weekend, anyway." one of his teammates sighed.

"Maybe, but maybe not," Gilbert said.

"What's going on here?" the coach asked as he approached everyone who was on the sidelines.

"We want to quit; we just keep losing!" one of the teammates said.

"I don't want you to quit; I want you to keep playing," Gilbert said.

Coach blew his whistle and called everyone together and started talking.

"Listen, I know we have not been doing so well, but that is no reason to give up.

Gilbert said something important earlier, and I think we should all listen to him. Gilbert, do you want to repeat what you said, please?" coach asked.

"I don't want you to quit; I want you to keep playing," Gilbert repeated.

"But why? We always lose!" another teammate protested.

"Because maybe we don't win, but that's okay! We have fun every week at practice, and we enjoy playing together. Just because we are not winning does not mean that we cannot have fun together. As my dad says: it's not about whether you win or lose; it's about how much fun you have trying." Gilbert said.

"Well said, Gilbert." coach said.

All of Gilbert's teammates agreed and mentioned how much fun they had when they were at practice every week.

"The games aren't so bad, either, it just sucks when we lose, and the other team is so mean about it." one of Gilbert's teammates said.

"I agree. Maybe we can just ignore them and celebrate by ourselves, though?" Gilbert suggested.

"Let's try that!" A teammate responded.

With their renewed sense of hope, Gilbert's entire soccer team practiced their best that day.

They dribbled the ball, scored goals, and blocked goals like they were professionals.

As they did, each of the team members cheered and celebrated each other loudly, which is something Gilbert had never seen them all do before.

The team was more spirited and excited than they had ever been before, and it was all thanks to Gilbert being willing to speak up and remind his team about what mattered.

When Saturday came, the teammates were all excited to play, and they did not care if they were going to win or lose.

Instead, they were just happy to be there playing at all.

They played a great game, too, scoring a few points and executing the plays that their coach had taught them to do perfectly.

The whole time they celebrated each other, cheered each other on, and high fived each other when they did a great job.

The morale of the team was at an all-time high, and it really showed in the way they played their game.

Even though they did not win that game, they did have a great time.

Afterward, they all stuck around long enough to enjoy juice and snacks that their coach had brought them as a reward for being such great team players.

The next week, they practiced even harder, and the team got even better at their plays, and at celebrating and cheering each other on.

They played their hardest all week long, and come that next Saturday game; they were feeling really good about themselves.

As the game began, everyone could tell that the team was already playing much differently than ever before.

Once again, they executed their plays perfectly and scored goals together.

The whole time, they celebrated each other, cheered each other on, and high fived each other.

They had so much fun playing that they almost forgot to pay attention to how many goals were being scored!

Toward the end of the game, the coach huddled everyone together and high fived everyone because they were winning.

The team was surprised and excited because this time, they did not care that they were winning; all they cared about was that they were having fun together.

The win felt like icing on the cake, but what really mattered was how good of a time they were having.

When the game was over, their coach and parents were so happy that they won that they agreed to take the entire team out for ice cream.

Everyone met at the local ice cream parlor and enjoyed a big double scoop of their favorite flavor, and as they did, they high fived and laughed and talked about how much fun they had at the game.

"So, how does everyone feel?" the coach asked as they were eating their ice cream.

"Great!" everyone responded.

"I thought I would care more about winning or that it would mean more to me, but I'm just really happy we all had fun." One of Gilbert's teammates said.

"Me too!" everyone agreed.

Together, they all agreed that from now on, they would play their best and that they would never put so much pressure on themselves to win ever again.

Instead, they would choose to have fun no matter what, and if they won, that would just be the icing on the cake.

I love how this story reminds me that winning is what life is all about. Sure, winning is fun, and it feels great, but life is not all about winning at things.

In fact, life has very little to do with winning anything at all.

Instead, life is more about enjoying yourself and having a great time with your friends and trusting that no matter what, you can always enjoy yourself.

If you choose to enjoy yourself, then you will not care if you win or lose because you will be too busy having fun.

Here are some great affirmations that can help you remember to choose to have fun no matter what, even if things are not going as planned:

"I am kind to myself."
"I remember that I deserve to have fun."
"I make things about fun."
"Life is about having fun."
"Today, I am going to have a lot of fun."
"I measure my success by how much fun I am having."

"I deserve to have fun."

"I love to have fun."

"I love having fun with people I love."

"I celebrate with the people I love."

Chapter 5: Penny Finds a Sunny Spot

This wonderful bedtime story is about a beautiful brown dog named Penny.

In this story, we are going to learn about Penny and how she has a wonderfully relaxing afternoon with her best friend, Boots, the cat.

Relaxing is such an important thing to be able to do, as it helps us have the energy that we need in order to get everything done on in our day!

In order to begin the story, we have to make sure that you are well-rested and ready to enjoy a wonderful night's sleep.

Begin by saying goodnight to your family, tucking yourself in, and getting comfortable in your bed.

If you need to have a drink of water or go to the bathroom, make sure you do that first!

Then, when you are ready, you can get started with the simple breathing meditation that we are going to do to help you prepare for a great sleep.

For this breathing meditation, you are going to focus on breathing in for a count of four and breathing out for a count of four.

Do your best to stay on track with my counting as you breathe in and out so that you can relax deeply, okay?

Let's begin.

Start by breathing into your tummy with a count of one, two, three, four.

Now, breathe all the way out, one, two, three, four.

Again, breathe in, one, two, three, four, and breathe out, one, two, three, four.

Now breathe in again, one, two, three, four, and breath out again, one, two, three, four.

Going onto your fourth breath now, breathe in, one, two, three, four, and breath out, one, two, three, four.

And one more time, breathe in, one, two, three, four, and breathe out, one, two, three, four.

Now that you are feeling nice and relaxed let's dig into this beautiful story about Penny, the dog, and her friend Boots, the cat.
Penny, the dog, is a beautiful brown dog.

Penny is about medium sized, reaching as high as her owner's knee.

She is a gentle, friendly dog who loves playing fetch and going for walks with her owner.

When she is not playing fetch or walking, Penny likes to take nice long naps at home with her friend Boots.

Boots is a black cat with little white "boots" on his feet.

Penny and Boots cuddle together when they nap, but otherwise, they tend to do everything else on their own.

Whereas Penny stays close to their owner, Boots likes to go for walks by himself and would rather chase a bird in the backyard than play fetch with their owner.

He lives a very different life from Penny, and yet they are best friends.

One day, Penny's owner took her for a walk and then dropped her off at home and left to go take care of some business.

Tired from her walk, Penny decided she was going to take a nap so that she could have enough energy to hang out with her owner again when he got home.

As she prepared for her nap, Penny first went and took a drink from her water bowl, then had a few bites of food from her food bowl.

Then, she started looking for Boots to let him know it was time for them to take a nap together.

Usually, Boots could either be found sitting in the kitchen window, playing in the basement, or napping in their owner's laundry basket.

Since she was already in the kitchen, Penny went over to the window and looked up, but Boots was not there.

Penny then walked through the kitchen, down the hallway, through the basement door, and down the stairs to see if she could find Boots playing with his toys in the basement.

She searched all three rooms down there, yet Boots was nowhere to be found.

Next, Penny went all the way back upstairs, back through the basement door, up the hallway, around the corner, up another flight of stairs, and down the hallway into their owners' room.

There, she saw the laundry basket, but it was empty.

Confused, Penny jumped up on their owners' bed and looked out the window into the backyard.

There, in the yard, Penny saw Boots chasing a bird.

Penny barked twice, and Boots looked up at her.

As he did, the bird flew away, and Boots looked cranky that Penny caused Boots to miss out on catching a bird.

Still, Boots made his way through the kitty door and into the house, and Penny ran downstairs to meet him in the kitchen.

When Penny came into the kitchen, Boots rubbed his head all over her, and she happily licked the top of his head as they greeted each other for the first time that morning.

The two then walked down the hall and into the living room to their bed in front of the living room window, where they always enjoyed a good afternoon nap together when their owner was away.

Penny first laid down on the bed in the spot where the sunlight was hitting, but Boots promptly came over and pushed Penny out of her spot.

So, Penny stood up and got out of their bed and waited on the floor while Boots made himself comfortable.

Boots stretched, curled up in the corner of the bed, then stretched out and took up most of the bed.

He was a bit of a bed hog, but Penny did not mind because that was still her best friend.

Happy to have her friend to snuggle with, Penny made her way into their bed and curled up in what was left of their cozy bed together.

As she laid there, Penny felt the warmth of the sunlight on her nose and the tip of her ears and felt the coziness of their bed all under her body.

After such a long walk with her owner, this felt really nice to help her relax and have the energy to do other things that day like play fetch and maybe even go for another walk.

As they laid there, Penny and Boots enjoyed a long nap by the living room window until their owner came home.

Learning how to relax is so important, and just because we are around our friends or loved ones does not mean that we cannot relax.

Taking the time to relax is a great opportunity to help calm your mind and your body so that you have the energy to do the things that you need to do every day.

Whether it has a nice relaxing sleep every night, or just taking a few minutes after school each day to sit down and relax after a hard day's work, relaxing is important.

In fact, relaxing is not only important for you, but it is important for everyone, too!

For example, I'll bet you see your parents relaxing often as they let their bodies and minds feel rested enough to do important things like taking care of you.

As you learn to relax just like Penny and Boots do, there are some great affirmations that you can enjoy to help you relax even better.

"I relax now."
"I let my entire body relax."
"I feel calm and peaceful."
"I make time for relaxation."
"Relaxing now helps me have more energy later."
"I am relaxed."
"I am calm."
"I am peaceful."
"Relaxing is helpful to me."
"I help other people relax."

Chapter 6: Josh and His Friend Make Amends

Sometimes in life, we do not agree with other people.

You might find yourself feeling frustrated with your family or friends, or even having an argument with them if you really do not agree about something.

Arguments can be stressful, and they can also lead to hurt feelings, too, if we are not careful.

In tonight's story, we are going to talk about a little boy named Josh and an argument he had with his friend, and how Josh and his friend made up so that they could keep being great friends.

Before we begin this story, you know what you have to do!

Make sure that you have done your whole night's routine, that you are feeling comfortable and peaceful, and that you are ready to relax into meditation and a great night's story.

Tonight, we are going to do a simple muscle relaxation to help you relax and get ready for bed.

This muscle relaxation is easy: I am going to tell you which part of your body to focus on, and you are going to squeeze your muscles in that part of your body as hard as you can for five seconds, then you are going to let go of them.

This way, you can completely release any energy you might have in your body so that you can have a comfortable and relaxing sleep.

Are you ready? Let's get started!

Begin by focusing on your feet.

Squeeze the muscles in your feet and toes as hard as you can for a count of five, one, two, three, four, five!

Okay, now release them completely and feel your feet muscles relaxing completely.

Now, let's do this for your legs, one, two, three, four, five!

Release your leg muscles and feel your legs completely relaxing into your bed.

Now, let's do this for your bum, one, two, three, four, five!

Let your muscles relax and feel yourself relaxing even more.

Now, your stomach, one, two, three, four, five!

Relax and feel yourself relaxing deeply.

Now, your chest, one, two, three, four, five!

Okay, relax your chest muscles and feel them feeling even more relaxed and peaceful.

Next, let's tense your arms up completely all the way down to your hands by making fists with your hands and squeezing your arms and hands as hard as you can for one, two, three, four, five.

Okay, now release your arms and hands and feel them relaxing into the bed.

Now, let's relax your neck and shoulders.

Squeeze your muscles in your neck and shoulders as hard as you can for one, two, three, four, five, and release.

Now, your head, squeeze the muscles in your head for one, two, three, four, and five, then release.

Now, your face muscles, squeeze your face muscles for one, two, three, four, and five.

Now, release.

The story of Josh and his friend Alex is an important one.

This is a story of two friends having an argument and then choosing to resolve that argument so they could continue to be great friends.

Let's start at the beginning so that you can understand why Josh and Alex were fighting in the first place.

Josh was having a wonderful day with his mom and dad and his little sister Katie.

Sometime in the early afternoon, is friend Alex called and asked if he wanted to come over and hang out.

Josh said yes, and his dad gave him a ride over to Alex's house so that they could play for the afternoon.

When he got there, Alex was playing with his blocks and his action figures.

Alex had made a big castle with his blocks and was pretending that his action figures were living inside of the block castle and were fighting over who would get to keep the castle and who would have to move away and make their own castle.

Josh thought this idea was great fun and tried to play with Alex when he arrived.

Josh picked up one of Alex's action figures and began playing, pretending that his action figure and Alex's action figure were fighting for who would get to have the castle.

At first, they were having fun, but then Alex began to get angry.

He said that Josh was not playing right and that he was making up stories that did not already exist.

Alex was having so much fun making believe on his own and playing his way that he had a hard time letting Josh have the chance to play with him.

At first, Alex tried to help Josh understand the game he was playing so that Josh could play it his way, too.

Josh did not want to play it Alex's way, though, because he was having more fun playing his way, and he did not really understand what Alex was trying to do, anyway.

Each time Alex tried to correct Josh and his style of playing, Alex got more and more angry with Josh.

Eventually, they began fighting over how they were playing, and Alex's mom decided maybe it was time for them to take a break.

Josh called his dad to pick him up, and Josh went back home for the evening.

Two days later, when they arrived at school, Josh was still feeling hurt by Alex.

He was upset that Alex had been so mean and that he was not letting Josh play his way, and Alex was still angry that Josh was not listening to him.

By the time recess came around, they were angry with each other, but they did not know who else to play with, so they tried playing together.

They tried playing together on the jungle gym, the swings, and even in the field.

Each time they tried to play a game, they would get angry and upset with each other.

Eventually, Josh got so angry that he declared he no longer wanted to play with Alex.

"You keep hurting my feelings and telling me that I cannot play or that I cannot have a say, and that is not fair. I do not want to play with you anymore!" Josh said.

"Fine, you don't know how to play properly anyway!" Alex argued.

Only, instead of walking away from each other, the boys kept shouting at each other.

By this time, their teacher came over and separated them.

"Maybe it is time you boys take a little break from each other."

Mr. Apple said as he encouraged the boys to play alone for a while.

Josh went away to play on the swings by himself, and Alex went away to the monkey bars on his own, too.

For the next two days, every time recess or lunch came around; the boys would play by themselves.

They were still angry with each other and hurt by each other's words and so they did not want to play together anymore.

By now, Josh's parents had noticed that he was no longer talking about or playing with his good friend Alex.

So, on the car ride home from school, his dad asked him what was going on.

"Why are you not playing with Alex anymore?" Josh's dad asked him.

"Alex, he's mean. He always tries to make the rules for how we have to play, and he never lets me play my way!" Josh said angrily.

"I understand." his dad said.

"Can you two not find a way to work it out and find a new way to play together where you both get to have a say?" he asked.

"No," Josh said.

When they got home that evening, Josh's dad called Alex's mom and invited them both over for dinner.

Josh was angry with his dad for inviting Alex over when he knew that he and Alex were no longer speaking.

When Alex and his mom came over, Josh refused to speak to him and instead sat quietly at the dinner table and ate the chicken that his dad had prepared for them.

"So, why are you two not talking?" Alex's mom asked.

"He never plays right!" Alex said, throwing his fork down.

"You never let me have a say!" Josh argued.

"Now, now, boys." Josh's dad answered.

"I think you two need to come up with a solution because I know you two are great friends.

One day, you will wish that you still had each other to play with if you do not make up now.

Remember all of the fun times you have spent riding bikes, playing in mud puddles, and swimming at the pool?" Josh's dad reminded them.

"Yeah." Josh and Alex responded.

"Alex, you need to apologize to Josh for not letting him make up any rules when you two are playing." Alex's mom said.

"Josh, I'm sorry that I never let you make up rules when we are playing. It's just, I like the way I play and the rules that I make up, and I want to do things my way sometimes." Alex said.

"It's okay, I understand. But sometimes I want to make up the rules, too. I like playing my way, too." Josh answered.

"Okay," Alex said.

"Josh, you need to apologize to Alex for saying that you do not want to play with him anymore." Josh's dad said.

"Alex, I'm sorry I said I did not want to play with you anymore."

"It's okay," Alex said.

The four of them then enjoyed a delicious chicken and rice dinner together.

As they ate, everyone made up great jokes and had a wonderful time.

Then, after dinner, Josh and Alex helped clean up the dishes and put them away.

Once they were done, they joined their parents in the living room.

"Alex, Josh, we need to have a talk." Alex's mom started.

The boys sat down in front of their parents and listened.

"Next time you are angry, you need to make sure that you stop and take care of it so that you do not hurt each other again, okay?" she said.

"Okay." the boys agreed.

"So, if you feel angry about something, you need to say why. And if you feel like you cannot get over your anger, or like you are arguing, you need to take a small break and then come back together and apologize for what you have done wrong. It is okay to make mistakes, but we must always apologize and own up to the things we have done in life. That way, we can help our friends feel better, and we can take care of our relationships with the people we love most. Understand?" Josh's dad asked.

"We understand." the boys said.

"Good."

After they had this talk with their parents, Josh and Alex went off to Josh's room to play with his new action figures.

They built a block castle and pretended to fight over who would get to keep the castle and who would have to go build their own.

Then, when they finally decided who had to go build their own, they both worked together to build the second castle so that they each had a great castle to play with.

This way, they both got to play together and have a good time and no one's feelings were hurt, and no one felt like they were being left out by the other.

From that point on, anytime Josh or Alex had an argument or hurt each other's feelings, they always took a small break and then apologized.

They went on to be the best of friends for many, many years, even watching their own children grow up playing together.

The value of friends is something that we must never take for granted.

When you have a great friend in your life, it is important that you always make up with them whenever you have a disagreement.

Just because you disagree with someone does not mean that you cannot still be friends with them.

It also does not mean that you should not tell that person how you feel if they have hurt your feelings.

Instead, take a little space and then be honest with that person about how they have made you feel.

Then, if you need to ask for forgiveness, make sure you ask.

If your friend asks for forgiveness, make sure you learn how to forgive them so that you can go on to be wonderful friends.

This is not just for friends, either, but for your family, too.

Everyone makes mistakes, and that is okay.

As long as we are willing to own up to our mistakes and make better choices in the future, we all deserve the chance to ask for forgiveness and do our best to make things better in the future.

If you ever find yourself in an argument with someone that you love, whether it is your friend or your parent, it is important that you always take the time to apologize if you have hurt someone's feelings.

You should also make sure that you forgive someone else if they hurt your feelings so that you can help yourself heal from how they have hurt you.

This way, you do not stay grumpy, but instead, you can find a way to be happy again, even after your feelings have been hurt.

Some great affirmations you can use to remind yourself to forgive others and ask for forgiveness when you have done something wrong are:

"It is safe for me to own my mistakes."
"I always apologize when I have hurt someone's feelings."
"I can always try better."
"There is room for improvement."
"It is okay to make mistakes."
"I forgive other people and their mistakes."
"I understand that people make mistakes."
"I can have compassion for people's mistakes."
"Friendship means more than a small argument."
"Family means more than a small argument."
"I can forgive others."

Chapter 7: Lisa Bakes a Cake

Tonight, we are going to enjoy a lovely story about my good friend Lisa, and the cake she baked with her dad!

This cake story is going to be so much fun; I know you will love learning about how to bake a cake with Lisa.

Before we can sink into a lovely story, though, we have to make sure that you are comfortable and relaxed enough to listen!

Make sure you have done your entire beautiful bedtime routine and that you are ready to lay completely still and listen to this story.

If you have not already, get a sip of water, say goodnight to your family, and get cozy in your bed.

Then, we can start with a nice and easy breathing meditation to help you calm your body down so that you can have a great sleep tonight.

Are you ready?

Let's begin with the simple breathing meditation.

For this meditation, I want you to imagine that you are holding a balloon in front of your face.

Can you do that for me?

Great!

Now, let's imagine that you are going to take a nice, deep, slow breath in through your nose, and then you are going to blow out through your mouth as if you were trying to fill the balloon up with air!

Starting now, breathe in nice and slowly through your nose, filling your lungs up with air.

Now, breathe out through your mouth as if you are trying to fill a balloon up with air!

Perfect, let's do it again.

Breathe in slowly through your nose, and now breathe out through your mouth to fill up your balloon.

Breathe in slowly, filling your lungs all the way up, and then exhale through your mouth, filling the balloon up with air.

Breathe in slowly, and once again breathe out filling up the balloon.

One more time, breathe in slowly through your nose, filling your lungs all the way up with air.

Now, breathe out through your mouth filling your balloon all the way up with air!

Perfect!

Now let's imagine that your balloon full of air floats away into the night sky, leaving you relaxed and ready to enjoy a wonderful story and a good night's sleep.

Goodbye, balloon!

One day, Lisa's dad told her that her mother's birthday was coming up!

Excited, Lisa started planning out what she could do for her mother's birthday.

Lisa was only eight years old, so it was not too easy for her to go to the store and pick out a lovely present to celebrate her mom.

So, she asked her dad to help her pick out a present and to help her bake a cake for her mom.

Of course, her dad said yes, and so in the week before her mother's birthday, Lisa's dad took her to the mall to pick out a present for her mother.

While there, Lisa picked out a beautiful silver necklace that said "mom" on it and had a heart shape around it with three rhinestones in the heart.

Lisa brought it home, wrapped it up, and hid it in her closet so that her mother would not find it before her birthday.

On the day of her mother's birthday, Lisa and her dad took to the kitchen to bake her mother a cake.

They started by gathering all of the supplies they needed.

"What do we need first, dad?" Lisa asked.

"Well, the recipe says that we need flour, sugar, cocoa, baking soda, and salt from the cupboard. Can you get those for us, kiddo?" Lisa's dad asked.

"Absolutely!" Lisa said.

Lisa went to the pantry, opened it up, and grabbed the flour from the bottom shelf, and the sugar, baking soda, and salt from the second shelf.

Then, she looked up and saw that the cocoa was all the way up on the top shelf.

"Can you grab it for me, please, dad?" Lisa asked.

"Great manners, Lisa! Of course, I can." her dad said, grabbing the cocoa off of the top shelf and putting it on the counter.

"What now, dad?" Lisa asked.

"Well, next, we need two eggs, buttermilk, butter, and vanilla." her dad answered.

"Great! I can do that!" Lisa said, opening the fridge to fetch the eggs, buttermilk, and butter.

"Where's the vanilla kept?" she asked, searching high and low for the vanilla.

"Whoops! That's in the cupboard!" her dad grinned, going back to the pantry to grab them the vanilla.

Lisa just giggled and grabbed a mixing bowl out of the cupboard.

"Is that everything?" Lisa asked.

"That is!" her dad smiled.

Lisa went back to the pantry, grabbed the footstool, and placed it by the counter where the mixing bowl was resting.

"Are we ready to get started?" she asked.

"We are! But first, we need the measuring cups and spoons! And a spatula." her dad said, pulling them out of the cupboard.

"Okay, let's get started!" he said.

"First, you need to measure out the flour. Can you measure out one and three-quarter cups of flour?" her dad asked, handing her the measuring cups.

"Absolutely!" Lisa said.

She carefully measured out the flour and dumped it into the mixing bowl.

"Great, now we need two cups of sugar. Can you put two cups of sugar into the bowl?" Lisa's dad asked.

"I sure can." Lisa grinned, adding two cups of sugar to the bowl. "Now, we need three-quarters of a cup of cocoa powder."

"Okay!" Lisa smiled, adding the cocoa powder to the bowl.

"Can you add one and a half teaspoons of baking soda now, Lisa?" her dad asked, handing her the measuring spoons.

"Of course!" Lisa said, measuring out the baking soda and adding it to the bowl.

"Great, now we need three-quarters of a teaspoon of salt."

"Got it!" Lisa said, adding the salt.

As she added the salt, a little spilled over onto the counter.

"Oops!" Lisa said, looking up at her dad.

"No problem." he smiled, wiping it away with a damp cloth.

"Now what?" Lisa asked.

"Well, it says here that now you need to mix the dry ingredients together."

"Okay!" Lisa answered, using the spatula to mix the flour, sugar, cocoa powder, baking soda, and salt together.

The mixture darkened as the cocoa powder blended in with the other dry ingredients and started to look like the packaged cakes that her grandma sometimes purchased when she did not want to make a cake from scratch.

"Great, that looks good, Lisa. Now, let's add the wet ingredients together. Let's start with the eggs." her dad said, handing her two eggs.
"Can you do it by yourself?" he asked.

"I sure can!" Lisa smiled, carefully cracking the first egg over the side of the mixing bowl.

The side split and Lisa used her fingers to pry the egg open, revealing a gooey egg white and yolk inside.

She dumped the egg into the bowl, and then placed the eggshell to the side.

She cracked in the next egg, again prying the gooey egg open and letting the egg white and yolk slide into the bowl next to the other egg.

This time, she accidentally got some shell into the bowl.

"Oops! How do I get that out?" Lisa asked.

"Check this out," her dad said, taking half of the empty eggshell and scooping the broken piece out of the batter.

"Woah, how did you do that?" Lisa asked, amazed by how easily her dad pulled the eggshell out.

"Baker's secret." he winked.

"Okay, now let's add the buttermilk, we need one and a half cups of that."

Lisa's dad said, handing her the buttermilk.

Lisa measured out the milk and then poured it into the mixing bowl, watching the thick white milk mix together with the eggs on top of the dry ingredients.

"Done," Lisa said, putting the measuring cup down.

"Great, now let's add the butter. We need to melt it first, so I will do that." her dad said, measuring out half of a cup of butter and placing it in a small pot over medium heat, stirring it regularly to help it melt.

Once the butter was melted, Lisa's dad added it directly to the mixing bowl.

"Now, the vanilla. This is the last ingredient!" he said, handing her the vanilla.

"How much?" she asked.

"One tablespoon." he smiled, handing her the measuring spoons once again.

"Excellent." she grinned, pouring a tablespoon of vanilla into the mixing bowl.

"That's it! Mix it up!" Lisa's dad said.

As she started mixing the bowl, her dad turned on the stove and prepared the cake pans.

Meanwhile, Lisa used the spatula to mix together the ingredients in the bowl.

At first, it seemed like they were not coming together that well, but Lisa kept mixing and mixing.

Soon, all of the ingredients were coming together in a soupy wet mixture.

The batter was fairly wet and thick, but it looked like it would be absolutely delicious once it was done.

When Lisa was satisfied that she had mixed it all the way through, her dad gave it one last mix just to be sure that it was perfect.

Then, they poured the mixture into two separate cake pans, and her dad put them in the hot stove for her.

Lisa was so excited to finish these cakes for her mother that she stayed in the kitchen the whole time they were baking.

She sat on the floor in front of the oven, watching them rise.

At first, it looked like nothing was happening as the cakes simply sat in the oven baking.

Soon, however, the smell of chocolate cake began to fill the house, and the cakes slowly began to rise.

Lisa continued sitting there, watching the entire baking process play out before her very eyes as both of the cake rose and baked all the way through.

When the oven went off, Lisa stood back as her dad pulled the cakes out of the stove and poked a toothpick into the center of them to make sure they were baked all the way through.

"Perfection!" he smiled, showing her the toothpicks were completely clean upon coming out of the cake.

Lisa's grandmother had taught her that this meant the cakes were cooked, but if the toothpick came out dirty with cake batter on it, they needed to be cooked a little longer.

They let the two cakes rest for a few minutes before turning them out onto a drying rack and letting them cool even longer.

Then, they iced the top of one cake and stacked the other cake on top of it.

"A double decker!" Lisa giggled, looking at the big, delicious chocolate cake they had made for her mother.

They iced the rest of the cake, then covered it in sprinkles and candles for her mother's birthday.

Then, they waited for her mother to get home.

When she did, they lit the candles and showed the cake to her mother, and her mother smiled and blew all of the candles out.

"You made this for me?" her mother asked, scooping Lisa up into a hug.

"Yes, dad and I did!" she answered.

"Here, we got this for you, too!" Lisa said, handing her mother the present they had bought her.

Lisa's mother opened the present and smiled when she saw the necklace.

"It's perfect," she said, hugging Lisa and her dad very close. "What a perfect birthday." Lisa's mother sighed.

The three of them ate the cake and enjoyed an evening laughing and playing board games together.

When you want to have something in your life, it can be helpful to know how to have the motivation to put the work in.

It might seem easier to go the convenient route and let someone else do all of the work for you, but then you do not get the special feeling of knowing that you did the work yourself.

Doing the work for yourself means that you get to feel proud of the work that you have done, and you get to share the special results with others.

The good feelings you have inside when you accomplish something special is important, and it can help you feel even better.

When you want something in your life but you are struggling to stay motivated to put the work in, remember these important affirmations:

"I can do it."

"I am capable of everything."

"I am great at making things happen."

"If I want it, I can create it."

"I can always try again."

"I am good enough."

"It is more special when I do it myself."

"I can always ask for help."

"Trying counts."

"One step at a time."

Chapter 8: Corey Hurts His Knee

Sometimes, not everything that happens in your life is a good thing.

Sometimes, you might find yourself feeling sad, angry, or even stressed out when you go through something in your life.

These feelings may be painful, but they are still important feelings to have.

Knowing how to recognize and honor your feelings is an important skill to have, and tonight's story is a great story about how you can do just that.

Before we get started, make sure that you have brushed your teeth, said goodnight to your family, and that you are tucked in for the night.

You want to make sure that you can rest completely so that you can have a great sleep tonight while you listen to this special story.

Once you are tucked in, we are going to do a nice and easy progressive muscle relaxation meditation, which is a skill that you can use to help you learn how to calm down your body.

This meditation is going to be easy: I will mention a part of your body, and you will simply focus on that body and let it relax.

When we are all done, your body will feel nice and comfortable, and you will be ready to enjoy a great sleep.

We are going to start this muscle relaxation with your feet.

I want you to imagine your feet feeling completely relaxed, as relaxed as they possibly can.

Imagine what they would feel like if they felt really, really peaceful.

Now, imagine that same peaceful feeling moving up through your legs, all the way up to your thighs.

Feel your thighs relaxing peacefully, as they start to fall all the way asleep.

Let that feeling move up into your hips now, relaxing all of your muscles along the way.

Feel your entire lower body from your hips to your toes, relaxing completely with this comfortable sensation moving through your feet, legs, and hips.

Now, let that relaxed feeling move up through your tummy.

Feel your tummy relaxing completely, and feel that relaxed feeling wrapping all the way around your lower back, too.

Let that feeling move up, as you feel your chest and upper back starting to relax completely now, too.

Now, see that feeling travel all the way down your arms, through your hands, and to your fingertips.

Feel your entire arms relaxing deeply, now.

At this point, your entire body from your shoulders all the way down through your belly, knees, and toes should be completely relaxed.

Now, feel that relaxing sensation moving up through your head, all the way through your face and hair as it relaxes you completely to the top of your head.

Now, from the top of your head to your toes, and from the bottom of your feet all the way to your forehead should be completely relaxed.

It's time to begin our story.

One day, a little boy named Corey was riding his bike.

Corey's bike was his favorite of all of his toys, and he rode it as often as he can.

He received it almost a year ago now for his birthday, and at the same time that he received the bike he learned how to ride it.

Back then, he was not very good at riding his bike.

He fell over a lot and sometimes had a hard time keeping up with the other kids when he was riding his bike.

As he rode it more and more, though, he got better and better at riding it.

Before he knew it, he could ride his bike as fast as any of the other kids, and as long as any of the other kids, without ever falling over.

Corey was so good at riding his bike that he was even learning some small tricks on it, like how to go over curbs or jump it over small jumps that he and his friends set up on their front lawns.

When Corey came home from school, he would immediately go to his bike and start riding it with his friends.

He rode his bike rain or shine, no matter what time it was until his parents told him it was time to come home for dinner or to go to sleep.

When he was done, Corey would put his bike away in the garage where he kept it and make sure that it was cleaned off and ready to go in the morning.

One day, in particular, Corey was excited to get home to ride his bike.

He knew his dad was going to be home that day, and he really wanted to show his dad the new tricks he had been learning on his bike.

After school, he rushed home and found his dad waiting for him, and they went straight to his bike so that Corey could show his dad the tricks he was most excited about.

When they were ready, Corey and his dad went out to the front lawn, and Corey started doing jumps over the curb on their driveway, and over the little jump, he had built in his front lawn.

He was so excited and proud to be showing his dad the tricks he had learned that he felt a little shaky and nervous, but he kept practicing and showing off anyway.

His dad celebrated with him, saying how cool the tricks were and how great of a job Corey was doing.

Wanting to impress his dad, Corey tried a more challenging jump that he had seen the older kids doing.

Corey had not tried this jump yet, but he thought he might be able to do it, and he really wanted to show his dad how good he was getting on his bike.

So, he went for the jump anyway.

Corey's dad watched, and Corey went over the jump, and then when he came down for the landing, his front tire turned, and Corey fell off the side of his bike.

When he landed, the handlebars had stuck him in the side, and he had skinned his knee.

Corey started crying and felt really upset about the pain he was feeling in his knee, as it began to bleed and sting.

Immediately, Corey's dad rushed over to him and scooped him off the ground into a big hug.

He picked up Corey's bike and took it to the house and brought Corey inside to take a look at his wound and see what he could do to help fix it.

Embarrassed and in pain, Corey started crying and hiding his face.

He felt bad that he was not able to do this jump for his dad, and he felt even worse that he was in pain.

"It's okay to not be okay, son." Corey's dad said, cleaning up his knee and putting Band-Aids over his cuts.

He then gave Corey a big hug and wiped away Corey's tears.

"I thought I could do it, but I had never tried it before. I really hurt myself, dad!" Corey said, crying into his dad's shoulder.

"It's okay to be sad when you hurt, Corey. You did a great try! Maybe next time you can watch the other kids again, and they can give you some tips on how to do an even better job next time." his dad said, hugging him even closer.

"David's mom said we should not cry because we are boys!" Corey said, hiding his face even more.

"That is not true; boys cry too." Corey's dad said.

"Even I cry sometimes," he added.

"You do?" Corey asked.

"Yes, I do. It is good to cry when we are sad, feeling our feelings is important. We should always honor our feelings when we feel them, no matter what we are feeling."

"Why?" Corey asked.

"Because your feelings tell you important things like what is right or wrong for you. When you feel your feelings, you give yourself the chance to actually heal from them. When you do not feel your feelings, they sit inside of you and feel worse until you cannot hold them inside anymore." Corey's dad said.

"What other feelings should I feel?" Corey asked.

"All of them! When you are sad or hurting, you should feel your feelings. When you are angry, frustrated, or upset, you should feel your feelings. When you are embarrassed, guilty, or ashamed, you should feel your feelings. When you are happy, excited, or surprised, you should feel your feelings. You should feel every single feeling you have, even if you think it is a good or a bad feeling. All of your feelings are important." Corey's dad said.

"I see," Corey answered.

By now, Corey was starting to feel better, and his knee was not stinging quite so much.

He wiped away his tears, sat back, and looked up at his dad.

"Why do some people think we should not feel our feelings?" he asked.

"I don't know." Corey's dad answered sighing.

"But I do know that your feelings are important, and you need to honor them whenever you feel them," he added.

"But what if my feelings feel strong, or I feel like hurting someone because my feelings are hurt?" Corey asked.

"Feeling and honoring your feelings do not always mean that you need to act on them, Corey.

You should always think before you act on your feelings to make sure that you are behaving in a way that will not hurt someone else.

Remember: hurting someone else will not make you feel better.

You should always tell people how you are feeling, and then find a way to feel your feelings in a way that is not hurtful to you or anyone else." Corey's dad said.

"I understand," Corey said.

"I'm feeling a lot better now, and my knee does not hurt so much. Thank you for helping me, dad." Corey said.

"You're welcome. Do you want to go try riding your bike again?" Corey's dad asked.

"Sure." Corey smiled, getting up and putting his helmet back on.

The two of them went back outside, and Corey rode his bike again.

This time, he rode it up and down the lawn, over small jumps, and over the curbs.

He did now, however, ride it over the big jump because he knew he was not ready for that, and that was okay.

Right now, he felt perfectly happy riding over the easier jumps that Corey knew he was good at and leaving the rest for another day.

Corey was still very proud of himself, and his dad was impressed by all of his tricks.

They had a wonderful afternoon playing together, and Corey felt much better about how to handle his own feelings from now on.

Feelings can be intense and overwhelming sometimes, and sometimes you may feel embarrassed about what you are feeling.

Remember, no matter how you are feeling, it is important to always honor your feelings.

Be truthful about how you feel, and tell people how you are feeling, especially if those people are causing you to have certain feelings.

When you do honor your feelings, make sure that you always think of ways to feel them that will be respectful and kind to yourself and others around you.

After all, acting unkindly due to a tough feeling will not help you feel better, but it may make you feel worse.

When you are dealing with tough emotions, here are some great affirmations that you can remember that might help you feel better as you go through them:

"It is safe for me to feel this way."
"I can honor my feelings."
"I can feel this way and still be kind."
"It is safe to talk about my feelings."
"It is okay to feel this way."
"I honor my feelings always."
"There is no such thing as a bad feeling."
"My feelings matter."
"I can express myself safely."
"Feelings can be felt by everyone."

Chapter 9: Pauline Needs a Break

Sometimes, when we are feeling overwhelmed or frustrated by life, a good break is important.

Maybe you have seen other people, like your parents, take breaks in life to help them feel better when they are feeling overwhelmed.

Maybe they had even helped you take a break before when you were feeling particularly overwhelmed.

No matter what the case may be, taking a good break is always important when you need one.

In tonight's story, we are going to talk about Pauline and how she needed a break, and what she did with her break to help her feel more relaxed after a stressful day.

Before we can get into our story, though, we need to make sure that you are relaxed and ready to have a great sleep!

Make sure you have said goodnight to your family, gotten a sip of water, and been tucked in for bed.

If you sleep with a favorite stuffed animal or blanket, make sure they are tucked in close with you and that you are all ready to focus on a wonderful dream tonight.

To help you calm down and relax, even more, we are going to use a special breathing meditation to help you have a great night's sleep.

This breathing meditation is an easy one, and it will help you feel far more relaxed.
If you are ready for this breathing meditation, let's begin.

For tonight's breathing meditation, you are going to imagine the air being filled with golden light that you will breathe in and breathe out as you relax.

This golden light is going to help you relax completely as you sink into a more peaceful feeling so that you can have a wonderful night's sleep.

You will start this meditation now by taking a nice deep breath in and visualizing golden light filling your lungs as you inhale and fill them up completely.

Then, you will visualize this golden light leaving your lungs as you exhale and completely release all of the air from your lungs.

Once again, you are going to breathe in nice and deep, visualizing golden air filling your lungs and helping you relax even deeper.

Now, exhale and visualize all of the golden air, leaving your lungs completely.

Again, breathe in and visualize this golden air filling your lungs, and exhale visualizing this golden air leaving your lungs completely.

Breathe in, visualizing golden light filling your lungs and helping you relax, then breathe out visualizing the golden air leaving your lungs and healing you relax.

One more time, breathe in and let this golden light fill your lungs, helping you to relax even deeper.

Then, breathe out, visualizing this golden light releasing from your lungs and helping you to relax even deeper.

Now, you are peaceful and ready for this wonderful story about taking a break when you need one.

Pauline was having an overwhelming time in her life.

Her family had recently moved, so everything was new to her.

Her bedroom, school, and neighborhood had all changed.

Pauline no longer recognized anyone she went to school with, and she had absolutely no friends where she came from.

She was overwhelmed and having a hard time settling into this new life that her parents sprung on her, seemingly out of nowhere.

It was very difficult for Pauline to feel like she belonged when everything seemed so out of place.

She missed her old friends, her old home, and her old neighborhood.

One day when she was still new at school, Pauline was having a particularly challenging day.

Her class was a little ahead of where her old school was, and she did not fully understand what her teacher was teaching her.

Her classmates were not as welcoming as they could be, which made it even more challenging for her to learn and catch up because she felt lonely and missed her old friends.

Pauline had a hard time finding her way and really felt overwhelmed and angry with all of the changes her parents had made.

On that day, in particular, Pauline was given a big homework assignment about a topic that she still felt was very confusing.

She was sure that she was not going to do well on that homework, and she felt worried that her parents would be upset with her for not doing so well.

She did not want to disappoint them, especially because they always told her about how proud they were of her being so smart and good in school.

Pauline was afraid that she would let them down and they would not be proud of her anymore if they realized she was no longer doing good in school.

She could not handle any more stress in her life, and this felt like way too much for her to handle by herself.

When she got home from school that day, her parents asked her how she was doing, and Pauline did not know what to say. "I'm feeling overwhelmed." she finally admitted, after being afraid, to tell the truth all along.

"Are you overwhelmed because we moved?" her mom asked.

"Yes, I don't know anyone here, my bedroom is all different, and my teachers are not that nice to me. This school is learning something brand new to me, and I just don't understand. They keep pushing it on me, and I am confused. To top it off, no one wants to study with me, so I cannot get help, and I am scared I will disappoint you. I am so sorry." Pauline said, burying her head into her hands.

"Don't be sorry, Pauline. We know you are going through a lot right now, and it is not easy. It is okay to feel overwhelmed. You are not disappointing us; you will never be disappointing us!" Pauline's dad said, giving her a hug.

"I know just what you need." Pauline's mom said.

"What?" Pauline asked.

"Wait here." Pauline's mom said.

Pauline sat with her dad, waiting as her mom disappeared upstairs, and when she came back, she told Pauline, "everything is ready for you!"

Confused, Pauline followed her mom upstairs.

When they got upstairs, Pauline saw that her mom had drawn her a bath so that she would have somewhere comfortable to relax.

The bath was full of bubbles, and a few candles were lit on the counter to help her have an even more relaxing time.

"This will help you feel better. When you are done, I will help you relax in your bedroom, too." Pauline's mom said, kissing Pauline on the forehead.

"It is okay to have a stressful time, and it is important to speak up for your needs just like you did now. You can take a break today; it is okay. Homework can wait." Pauline's mom smiled, leaving the room.

Pauline climbed into the tub and laid back, watching as the bubbles covered over her and listened as they made popping noises in her ears.

She laid there for several minutes as the candles flickered, and the light danced on the walls, and she thought about how much she missed her home, and her friends, and her school.

She continued laying there until she did not feel quite so overwhelmed anymore, and then she climbed out of the tub, dried off, and drained the water out of it.

When she got out of the bathroom and went into her bedroom, Pauline saw that her mom made her bedroom relaxing, too.

Her bed was made up with comfortable sheets, her favorite stuffed bunny was on the bed next to her pillows, and her mom had left a small plate of snacks and a drink of milk in the room for her.

"How are you feeling now?" her mom asked, coming into her room.

"I'm okay; I'm still overwhelmed, though," Pauline said.

Pauline's mom gave her a hug and helped her into her bed, and gave her the snack of cookies and her milk.

"Relax here; it will help you feel better. Sometimes, a time out can help our mind come to terms with everything that is happening so that you can begin to feel more at peace with your life." Pauline's mom explained.

"Okay," Pauline answered.

"I will be back later, you enjoy your break and do not worry about homework or anything, just relax." Pauline's mom smiled.

Pauline laid back in her bed and looked out her window as she snacked on cookies and drank her milk.

She laid on her bed, wondering what her friends were doing and wondering what school was like at her old school that day.

She wondered if anyone was missing her, too, and if she would ever see her friends again.

For a while, she continued to feel overwhelmed and stressed out by how much she missed everyone from her old school.

Pauline had a very difficult time coming to terms with all of these feelings and everything that she was going through from this move.

She started to feel angry again, too and upset with her parents for making her leave behind her best friends.

She could not understand how her parents could do this, or why they would do this, and she felt like nothing would ever be the same again.

"How are you doing?" Pauline's dad asked when he came into her room to check on her.

"I'm angry; why would you make us move away? I miss my friends!" Pauline said, pouting into her comforter.

"I know you do not understand, Pauline, but this was move was for the best. Right now, you miss your old friends and your old school, and that is okay. But one day, you might become excited about your new school. There are new friends here waiting to play with you, and I know you are going to meet them soon. Have you met any yet?" he asked.

"No, I haven't! I don't want new friends; I want *my* friends!" Pauline protested.

"I know, Pauline. I'm sorry we had to move." Pauline's dad answered.

"I still think you will find that one day you will become curious about who you will meet here, and what you and your new friends will do together. Can you do me a favor? Tomorrow when you go to school, try being curious about what new friends you could make and what life might be like when you settle in."

"I'll try," Pauline said, sadly.

"Okay." Pauline's dad gave her a hug and left the room, letting her relax once again.

As Pauline sat there, she started going from angry to curious.

She wondered if her dad was right and if she would make new friends here.

She wondered if anyone would like her and if she would get along with anyone as good as she did with her old friends.

Soon, she grew tired, and she laid down and fell asleep for a nap.

By the time she woke up, Pauline was starting to feel much better.

That day at school, Pauline went in with a curious mind as her dad asked her to.

She was curious about who she might meet, what friends she might have, and what life might be like with her friends.

As she did, she realized that there were actually a lot of really fun people at her new school.

She met two new friends, and she felt much happier and more relaxed than she did in days.

"Maybe things won't be so bad after all." Pauline thought to herself, as she ate lunch with her new friends.

When she got home from school, Pauline told her mom and dad about the new friends she made.

"You were right; I did make new friends! I feel much better now; I really think that break yesterday helped me a lot. Thank you." Pauline said.

"I knew you would!" her dad smiled.

"You're welcome." Pauline's mom said, kissing her forehead and giving her a big hug.

Sometimes, life can be stressful and overwhelming.

When we are stressed or overwhelmed, it feels harder to do things because you are too wound up.

Taking a good break can help you clear your mind, release your stress and feel ready to do the things you need to do in life.

Sometimes, taking time out and having a good break is the best thing you can do for yourself.

It is always important to recognize your needs and honor them so that you can do things in your life without feeling so stressed out or overwhelmed.

When you do find yourself feeling stressed out or overwhelmed, or needing to respect and honor your own needs, here are some affirmations to use to help you:

"My needs are important."

"It is safe to say not right now."

"No is a complete answer."

"I can take a break."

"Breaks are important."

"My needs matter."

"It is safe to take a break."

"I can fulfill my needs."

"I can ask for help."

"I can be honest about what I need."

Chapter 10: Devon Tries Again

Learning something new can be challenging.

You might worry that you are not as good at what you are trying to do as the people who have been doing it longer than you have been.

Part of becoming good at something is learning how to try again, even when you make a mistake so that you can learn to get better at your new skill.

In tonight's story, that is exactly what we are going to talk about.

Let's start tonight with a gentle progressive muscle relaxation skill so that you can let your body completely relax and fall asleep while you listen to this story.

To do this meditation, all you have to do is focus on the parts of the body that I tell you to focus on and let yourself relax completely.

As you learn to relax each part of your body, you will find yourself relaxing easier and faster every time, which will help you fall asleep even easier going forward.

Before you start your muscle relaxation, make sure that you have said goodnight to your family, brushed your teeth, and gotten comfortable in bed.

Once everything is ready for you to say goodnight, you can start this relaxation, and we can share a bedtime story together!

To begin your muscle relaxation, I want you to focus from the bottom of your feet all the way up to your knees.

Kindly ask every muscle in this area of your body to relax completely so that you can have a wonderful night's sleep.

Feel the muscles relaxing as they sink deeper into the bed and relax completely.

Now, focus from your knees all the way up to your hips.

Feel every single muscle in this area of your body relaxing completely as you let yourself sink deeper into your bed and grow more comfortable for a cozy night's sleep.

Next, focus on your hips all the way up to your belly button.

Let every muscle in this area of your body relax, as you kindly ask it to prepare for a wonderful sleep.

Now, focus on your belly button all the way up to your shoulders, and your shoulders all the way down to your fingertips.

Ask all of the muscles in your chest and arms to relax completely and feel them sinking deeper into your bed as you relax completely.

Now, focus on the space between your shoulders and the top of your head.

Ask all of the muscles in your neck, face, and head to relax completely so that you can have a wonderful sleep tonight.

When you feel all of your muscles from the top of your head to the bottom of your feet relaxed, we can start your bedtime story.

Devon was a very nice boy.

He listened to his parents, was nice to his sister, and got good grades in school.

He knew how to help the neighbors mow their lawns, he always helped elders walk their groceries to their car, and he loved sharing his snacks with his neighborhood friends.

Ever since he was little, his parents would always tell Devon what a nice boy he was and how helpful he was.

Devon loved knowing that he was nice and always strived to be nice to all of the people he met.

One day, Devon's parents decided to move to a new neighborhood where they would be closer to his parent's work.

There, he would also attend what they said was a better school.

Plus, because he was ten years old now, he would help his sister get to and from kindergarten to help his parents and help her have a wonderful day at school.

Devon was excited about all of the new responsibility he would get, and all of the new things he had to look forward to.

While he knew he was going to miss his old friends and old school, his parents assured him that he would get to see his old friends anytime he wanted on weekends and school breaks.

So, even though he was a little scared, Devon was mostly excited to make new friends and enjoy a new school.

On his first day at his new school, Devon woke up, got himself dressed, and brushed his teeth.

He combed his hair, put all of his books in his bag, and sat down to eat breakfast with his little sister Christy.

Once they were done eating, his mom packed up Christy's bag, too, and got her ready to go to school.

When the time came, Devon hugged his mom goodbye and carefully walked Christy to school.

He was sure to stop at all of the crosswalks, look both ways, and help her to safely cross the road.

They made it all the way to school before the bell rang, and he dropped her off at her kindergarten class and showed her where he would pick her up when school was over.

After he dropped Christy off at kindergarten, Devon went to find his own class.

He remembered where it was because his parents had just brought him and Christy there to tour their new school the weekend before.

So, he made his way to class and got himself ready for the day.

His new teacher, Mr. Stokes, helped Devon find his cubby and his desk and helped Devon get ready for their first class.

Devon was excited, and he was sure he would make many new friends at this wonderful new school.

As the minutes ticked by, kids started piling into the class and sitting at their desks all around him.

Each one of them seemed to come in with a group of friends and sat down together, talking amongst themselves.

Not one person talked to Devon, and Devon wondered if they could even see that he was there.

"Did no one realize that there was someone new in class to talk to?" Devon wondered.

By the time recess came, Devon was still spending his time alone.

Everyone left the room in their groups of friends, and Devon walked out by himself.

When he got to the playground, Devon looked around him and realized that everyone had a group of friends to hang out with except him.

So, Devon went up to a group of friends that seemed to be having fun and tried to play with them.

He tried playing with them on the monkey bars, on the swings, and on the slides.

Devon tried playing with them in the field, and on the playground, and in the courtyard.

No matter how hard he tried, no one ever wanted to play with Devon, they simply kept pushing him away or running away from him.

Devon felt sad.

The bell rang, and Devon made his way back to class, alone.

He sat in class alone and did his work alone.

Then, lunchtime came.

This time, Devon tried to play with a different group of friends, but the same thing happened.

Each time he tried to play with them, the friends would run away, and Devon would be left playing by himself.

He started to feel lonely and wondered if something was wrong with him or if there was a reason why no one wanted to play with him at his new school.

Devon felt sad.

By the end of the day, Devon felt like maybe his new school was not so wonderful after all.

He went and picked up his sister Christy from kindergarten, and they walked home.

When they got home, Devon's mom asked how their day was.

Christy told her about how great it was and how many new friends she made, and showed their mom the craft they made in kindergarten.

Devon sighed and said, "It was no fun! I tried making friends, but no one wanted to play with me. It's like they did not even see I was there."

Devon's mom sat down next to him and said: "walk me through it. What did you do when you tried to make new friends?"

"Well, I walked up to them and started playing. I played the way they were playing, but no one ever included me. They just kept running away!"

"I see." Devon's mom said, hugging him.

"Tomorrow, why don't you try introducing yourself first? Maybe these children just wanted to know who you were and they did not know how to ask." his mom suggested, giving him one last squeeze.

"I guess so," Devon said.

"Keep trying, honey, making friends can be hard. You will get better at it; it takes practice." his mom assured him.

Then, she got them an afternoon snack, and they played in the backyard for the rest of the afternoon.

The next day, Devon got himself ready for school again.

He carefully walked Christy all the way to kindergarten, making sure to stop and look both ways at the crosswalks and taking his time getting her there safely.

Then, he made his way to his class.

This time, he sat there, ready to make new friends right away.

When the first group of kids walked in the door, he stood up and went over to them.

"Hello, my name is Devon!" he said, smiling.

Everyone was quiet and kept walking to their desks, except one kid who said, "Hello Devon! I'm Scott!"

Devon smiled and perked up, realizing that someone had answered him and had noticed he was there.

"Hi Scott!" Scott kept walking to his desk.

"This is Patrick, Lenora, Silas, and Alyssa," Scott said, pointing at the other kids who walked into the room with him.

They all smiled and waved at Devon, and Devon waved back.

Devon sat at a desk near the group, and he and Scott talked, and Devon learned that not long ago, Scott was the new kid, too.

Scott explained that it was hard to make new friends at first, but then he began to feel like he fit in and now he had great friends.

Devon felt inspired by Scott and hoped that he would have the same wonderful experience at his new school.

When class started, they all sat together, and Scott helped Devon understand the work they were doing in class.

Then, when recess came, Alyssa invited Devon to come play with them.

At lunchtime, Silas and Patrick offered to trade lunch items with Devon because he was not a big fan of the lunch his mom had packed him.

At the end of the day, Devon learned that Lenora lived near him and so she walked home with Devon and Christy.

Devon started to feel a lot better as he realized that making friends was not as hard as he thought; it just took practice.

When he got home, Devon's mom asked him how his school day went.

"Did you make any new friends?" she asked.

"I did! I made new friends with Scott, Patrick, Silas, Lenora, and Alyssa. Lenora even lives close by and walked home with Christy and me!" he grinned.

"I knew you could do it. Did introduce yourself help?" his mom asked.

"It did! At first, only Scott talked to me, but then everyone started talking to me, and we all played together at recess and lunch."

"It sounds like today went much better." his mom smiled.

"It did." Devon smiled back.

Sometimes, trying something new, like making friends, can be challenging.

You might find yourself feeling overwhelmed or struggling to do what you set out to accomplish.

It is normal to feel afraid or overwhelmed when you are trying something new, which is what causes you to feel afraid to try again.

The good news is if you keep trying, you can only get better.

Giving yourself a chance to try again is a wonderful opportunity to make sure that you can do better next time.

As you try new things and prepare to try again, here are some wonderful affirmations to help you along the way:

"Trying again is important."
"Trying again is how I get better."
"Improvement comes from trying again."
"I can do better next time."
"Each time I try, I get better."
"Practice makes improvement."
"I can learn new skills."
"I can do this."
"I can always try again."
"It is okay to try again."

Chapter 11: David Goes Whale Watching

Have you ever wondered what it would be like to head out to the sea and go whale watching with your family?

Whale watching is a wonderful experience that is enjoyed by many who live near the beautiful ocean.

In tonight's story, we are going to talk about how David went whale watching with his family and all of the wonderful experiences he had and the emotions he learned about as he went.

Before we start our story, make sure that you are ready for bed!

Say goodnight to your family, brush your teeth, and get a drink of water.
If you have a favorite blanket or stuffed animal, you like to sleep with, snuggle up close with them and get ready for a wonderful night's sleep.

Then, when you are ready, we can spend a few minutes breathing to help you relax with a calming meditation before we start tonight's story.

That way, your body is nice and relaxed and ready to stay still while you listen to the story and prepare yourself for a wonderful dream.

For this breathing meditation, we are going to breathe in for the count of five, hold it for two seconds, and breathe out to the count of seven.

This helps you relax your mind, and it tells your body that it is time to calm down and go to sleep.

You can start this meditation when you are ready by breathing to the count of one, two, three, four, five, holding it for one, two, and breathing out for one, two, three, four, five, six, seven.

Again, breathe in for one, two, three, four, five, hold it for one, two, and breathe out for one, two, three, four, five, six, seven.

Breathe in again for one, two, three, four, five, hold it for one, two, and breathe out for one, two, three, four, five, six, seven.

Breathe in for one, two, three, four, five, hold your breath for one, two, and let it out for one, two, three, four, five, six, seven.

One more time, breathe in for one, two, three, four, five, hold it for one, two, and let it go for one, two, three, four, five, six, and seven.

Now, let your breath go back to normal as you settle in for a wonderful story about David and his whale watching experience.

David was so excited to go visit his family on the coast.

He spent the whole week packing his bags.

He packed his pants, his shirts, his underwear, his socks, his shoes, and even a few of his favorite toys.

In a smaller bag, he packed his toothbrush, toothpaste, shampoo, conditioner, and a small towel.

All of his bags were ready to go on Friday morning when it was time for him and his parents to make the drive to the coast where they would stay with David's grandparents for the weekend.

David was so excited to see his grandparents as he had not seen them in months, and he missed them dearly.

The whole way there, he excitedly talked about what they would do, how they would spend their time, and what fun it would be to spend this weekend with his grandparents.

To help him contain his excitement, his parents encouraged him to play games like counting how many telephone poles he saw in one town, or counting how many green cars he saw along the way.

David played along and counted out 19 telephone poles, and 37 green cars.

After what seemed like forever, David and his parents arrived at the coast and at his grandparent's house.

His grandparents were just as excited to see him as he was to see them, and they enjoyed a wonderful evening eating his grandma's delicious spaghetti and meatballs with a slice of cake for dessert.

That night, he slept in the guest room with a big smile on his face because he was so excited to be with his grandparents again.

When the next morning came, David woke up and saw that his grandparents and his parents were packing some bags.

"Are we leaving already?" David frowned.

"No, not at all. We are going on an adventure today!" David's grandpa exclaimed.

"An adventure? Where?" David asked.

"It's a surprise." his grandpa grinned.

"Before the adventure, you need a good breakfast to help you get started with your day!

Come on, let's enjoy some pancakes and bacon before we leave." David's grandma said, calling everyone into the dining room.

Everyone went and ate their breakfasts, and it was delicious.

When they were done, they cleaned their plates.

"Is it time for the adventure now?" David asked.

"It sure is!" his grandpa grinned, giving him a thumbs up.

David, his parents, and his grandparents all got their shoes on and got ready to leave the house.

While they were on their way to the adventure, David felt excited and confused.

He had no idea what they were getting up to, but he knew it was going to be a good time because he always had fun with his grandparents.

As they drove, David started to see the ocean in front of them.

He could see it getting bigger and bigger as they drove closer.

"Are we going to the beach?" he asked.

"Sort of." his mom said, keeping their adventure a mystery.

David grew even more curious as they drove closer and closer to the beach, and eventually parked in a parking lot near the water.

146

"We are going to the beach, aren't we?" he said, excited.

"You'll see." his dad grinned.

His parents and grandparents picked up some of the bags out of the trunk and locked the car as they began walking toward a small building on the beach.

When they got there, David saw tons of pictures and statues of whales on the building.

"What are we doing, grandpa?" he asked, looking around in wonder.

"We're going whale watching!" his grandpa responded.

"Whale watching? I have never been! This is so exciting!" David said, jumping all around.

His parents and grandparents smiled as they checked in, and everyone got ready to go whale watching.

When they were all checked in, one of the guides leads David and his family to the boat that they would use to go whale watching.

Each of them climbed aboard and found a seat to sit on as they relaxed and watched out toward the sea.

David was so excited about what was going on that he could hardly contain himself, but the whale watching guide told him it was important that he sit down and stay still so that he does not accidentally hurt himself or fall off the boat.

Then, the guide handed each of them life jackets and told them what to do if they did fall out of the boat or if anything happened.

He assured them that it was unlikely that anyone would fall out, but that it was important that he tell them what to do anyway just in case.

As David listened to the guide, he looked over the edge of the boat and realized how far away the water was.

He started to grow scared as he realized what might happen if he moved, so he sat incredibly still.

In fact, he sat so still that David's grandma wondered if something was wrong.

"Are you okay?" she asked.

"I am, I am just scared of falling into the water. I have never fallen into the ocean before, what if I get hurt?" he asked.

"You will be okay, just stay relaxed and close to grandpa and I and we will keep you safe." David's dad assured him.

He was sitting between his dad and grandpa, and, realizing that he was not alone, he started to feel more comfortable.

For the first little while out on the water, David felt scared.

He worried that something might happen and that they would get hurt.

Once they had been out for a while, though, David began to settle down.

He relaxed so much that he was able to laugh at the jokes that his grandpa was telling as they enjoyed the view and a wonderful time together.

Soon, they made it to the point where the whales were, and the guide told them to look up.

David looked out where the guide was pointing and saw the backs of whales as they bobbed through the water.

149

They seemed to be playing and dancing in the waves as they swam around.

One even sprayed water up into the air higher than their boat!

The guide carefully moved the boat a little closer so that they could get a better view.

David was surprised by how beautiful and fascinating the whales were to watch.

When he asked to go closer, the guide told him they had to stay further away so that the whales did not get hurt.

The guide said that sometimes the whales became so curious about the boats they would come to touch them with their noses, and they might get hurt by the propellers.

David did not want the whales to get hurt so he agreed they should keep their distance and enjoy the whales from afar.

They sat there for a while and watched the whales dancing in the waves as they enjoyed the sunlight.

It seemed as though they were all playing together, and David thought that was cute.

After a while, the whales began to disappear.

The other boats that had also been whale watching began to head back toward shore, and their guide suggested that David's family start going back toward shore, too.

"Aw, but I don't want to! I'm having fun!" David said.

"I know, but we have to say goodbye to the pod of whales and let them have a good sleep!" David's mom said.

"What is a pod of whales?"

"A pod is what you call a group of whales." his mom answered.

"Oh. Bye pod of whales!" David said, waving at the whales.

The guide began to take David and his family back to shore.

When they got there, they took their life jackets off and one by one they got off the boat.

His parents went to talk to the guide while David and his grandparents brought their bags back to the car.

When his parents were done talking, they all got back into the car and started to head back to his grandparent's house.

Slowly, the ocean grew further and further away as they went back toward the suburbs where his grandparents lived.

Before he knew it, they were back home and ready to enjoy a wonderful dinner together.

David was tired, but he stayed awake long enough to enjoy dinner with his grandparents and his family.

When dinner was ready, they all sat down together at the table and enjoyed a wonderful meal.

They had ham, mashed potatoes, carrots, gravy, corn, and buns.

When that was done, David and his family enjoyed another slice of his favorite cake for dessert, and David even got to have a few of the cookies his grandma often ate with her tea after dinner.

As they were sitting down enjoying the evening, his grandma asked: "David, what was your favorite part of today?"

"My favorite part was seeing the pod of whales playing in the waves. It looked like they were dancing! And when the whale sprayed water into the air!" David said, making a grand gesture into the air as if he were the whale spraying water.

David's parents and grandparents giggled as they watched him act out the part of the whales.
When he was done, David sat down on the couch and began to fall asleep.

"Are you tired?" his mom asked.

"Yes," David whispered.

David's dad carried him to the guest room where he was tucked in so that he could enjoy a wonderful night's sleep after a great day of whale watching with his family. The end!

Going on adventures can be fun, but they can also sometimes be scary.

When you do not know what you are doing, it can be scary to try new things.

The good thing is, you do not have to go on adventures alone, and you can always rely on your loved ones to help you feel safe.

When you know that you are going to be safe while going on an adventure, adventures can be great fun and can lead to wonderful lifelong memories.

You may not realize it now, but these memories will be very special to you!

As you test out new adventures in your own life, I encourage you to keep these affirmations close by to help you feel confident when taking adventures:

"It is safe to go on adventures."
"Adventures with my family are fun."
"Trying new things is great."
"I feel my feelings when I try new things."
"Adventure is fun."
"I love adventures with my family."
"I listen to the rules when I go on adventures."
"Listening to the rules helps me stay safe."
"Adventures can be a great time."
"These memories will last forever."

Chapter 12: Daffodil Meets a Friend

Learning how to make friends is a wonderful skill to have in life.

Making new friends can be hard, especially if you feel shy or afraid of talking to groups of new people.

Whenever I am feeling shy or afraid of making new friends, I always think about the story of Daffodil, the fairy.

Daffodil was a fairy who wanted a new friend but was unsure about how to make any.

When she learns, though, she feels much better knowing that now she has a friend that she can play with every day, just like the other fairies did!

To help you get ready for storytime, let's make sure that you have completed your entire bedtime routine.

Make sure you have brushed your teeth, had a sip of water, gone to the bathroom, said goodnight to your friends, and tucked yourself into bed.

You should also make sure your light is off so that you can have a great sleep!

Once you are all tucked in and ready for bed, you can start tonight's meditation using a wonderful muscle relaxation skill that will help you feel more at peace in your life.

Are you ready? Let's begin!

Start your relaxing muscle meditation by focusing on your feet, your ankles, your legs, your knees, and your hips.

Thank your feet, ankles, legs, knees, and hips for helping you walk through the day, and ask them to relax completely.

Now, they can have a wonderful rest from all of the running, jumping, climbing, and hopping you did so that they have plenty of energy to play again tomorrow.

Next, let's focus on your belly.

Thank your belly for helping you eat all of the wonderful food you ate today and for helping you drink all of the wonderful drinks you had today, and then ask it to have a wonderful rest.

Let it relax completely as you prepare for your sleep.

Now, let's focus on your chest.

Thank your chest for allowing you to breathe and for filling up with air and helping your heart beat.

Then, ask it to relax so that you can have a wonderful night's sleep.

Feel your breath helping you relax as you breathe in and out.

Now, let's focus on your shoulders, arms, elbows, wrists, hands, and fingers.

Thank your shoulders, arms, elbows, wrists, hands, and fingers for helping you pick up, grab, lift, carry, and climb through the day.

Ask them to relax completely so that they can have plenty of rest and energy for a brand new day tomorrow.

Now, let's focus on your neck and head.
Relax all of the muscles in your neck and head as you thank them for helping you think, speak, see, and smell all day long.

Let them relax completely so that they, too, can have a wonderful rest.

Once you have asked all of your body to rest and you have thanked it for all of the work it has done, you are ready to start your story about Daffodil, the fairy, and her new friend Daisy.

Daffodil was an adorable fairy.

She was no more than the size of your pinky finger, and she was quite the lovely little friend, indeed.

Daffodil had yellow hair and pale skin, and she wore a beautiful white dress made of petals.

Her wings looked like sparkling leaves, and they helped her fly through the forest like a master.

Daffodil loved flying, almost as much as she loved baking and bowling with small berries from the forest.

One day, as she was flying through the forest and playing with the butterflies, Daffodil realized that she was pretty lonely.

She wanted friends, but all of the other fairies in the forest seemed to already have friends.

She noticed that she was always alone while the other fairies played with each other and had a wonderful time together.

This made Daffodil feel sad and left out because she wanted to be a part of the fun.

Instead of letting her sadness get to her, Daffodil decided that she wanted to make a friend, too.

She was not going to be the only fairy with no friends anymore; she wanted to have someone to play with who would love playing bowling and flying around with the butterflies as much as she did. So, Daffodil set out to meet new friends.

Daffodil searched high and low for new friends.

She flew around the forest, went to the local waterholes, and checked all of the berry patches where fairies always got their food from.

She checked the homes of frogs and turtles, and flew around the creek, and yet everywhere she went, all she saw were groups of fairies who seemed too busy to pay her any attention.

Daffodil was too scared to go up to an entire group of fairies to try to make friends, so instead, she stayed to herself that day.

She felt sad that by the end of the day, she did not have a single friend.

Daffodil wondered if she would be lonely forever, or if she would one day find a friend who wanted to play with her.

When she got home that night, Daffodil made herself a supper of berries and berry juice and sat by her fireplace and relaxed.

This night was different from the other nights, though.

She did not feel energized and happy because she spent the day playing with butterflies, but instead, she felt sad and alone because she could not find a single fairy that she could play with.

Daffodil felt sad when she went to bed that night, and she felt sad when she woke up in the morning.

Still, she was not going to let her sadness or loneliness stop her, Daffodil wanted to make friends, and so she would try again on this new day.

This time, Daffodil went to all of the same places.

She flew around the berry fields, the frog and turtle homes, and the creek.

She went to the places where all of the faeries hung out, and once again, all she saw were groups of fairies hanging out and playing.

They were laughing, giggling, joking, dancing around, and playing with the animals of the forest.

Daffodil seemed to be the only one who was all by herself, except for the elder fairies who were all relaxing on their patios and enjoying time alone, as they often did in their elder years.

Feeling defeated, Daffodil went to visit her favorite elder, Elder Sage.

Elder Sage was an older fairy who had been living in the forest for many years and had a great deal of knowledge to offer Daffodil about life every time they talked.

Hoping for some advice, Daffodil sat down with Elder Sage on her patio and explained her problem about not being able to find anyone to be friends with her.

This time, rather than giving her advice, Elder Sage mentioned she had a new niece in the forest who was also looking for a friend.

She, too, was having a hard time fitting in with any of the groups and felt lonely in the forest.

Elder Sage set up a time where Daffodil would meet her niece, and then the two simply sat around and enjoyed a cup of berry tea as they watched everyone play and enjoy the sparkling sunshine.

The next day, Daffodil showed up at the creek where Elder Sage told her to show up, and when she arrived, another fairy was already sitting there.

Daffodil flew over to the fairy and introduced herself.

"Hi, my name is Daffodil!" she said, smiling.

"Hi, I am Daisy!" the other fairy said.

Daisy was dressed in a yellow and white dress and had brown hair and beautiful sparkling wings that looked like leaves, just like Daffodil did.

"Do you want to play with me?" Daffodil asked.

"Sure!" Daisy giggled.

The two fairies began flying around the forest, chasing butterflies, singing to birds, and playing with the frogs.

They flew into little caves in the forest and played hide and go seek, they skipped on the creek, and they played in the berry fields where they picked berries for dinner.

When they were done, they went back to Daffodil's house, and they prepared a delicious berry soup for dinner.

They enjoyed the berry soup on her patio and watched the sun as it danced across the sky, preparing for sunset.

"This day has been so much fun!" Daffodil smiled.

"I agree!" Daisy said.

"I was feeling so lonely; it can be hard to make friends sometimes. It seems like everyone else already has friends, and I'm always the one left out. I'm so glad I met you!" Daffodil said.

"I'm glad I met you, too! I am new here, and I thought I would never make friends." Daisy said.

The two girls smiled and finished their berry soup.

When they were done, they took their bowls inside and washed them, and put them away in the cupboards.

Then, they took some of the pigment from the berries and went back outside to paint the sunset as it cast over the sky.

When it got dark, Daisy said it was time for her to go home.

"Do you want to have a sleepover?" Daffodil asked.

"Sure!" Daisy said.

Instead of going home for the night, Daisy went to her house and grabbed her pajamas, and then came back to Daffodils to enjoy a sleepover.

The two fairies watched movies, painted their nails, and chatted all night about how wonderful it was to play with the butterflies and the birds and live in such a beautiful forest.

They also hung their paintings on the wall so that Daffodil's house looked even cozier.

When they were tired, the two curled up and went to sleep and enjoyed a lovely sleep.

As she was falling asleep, Daffodil thought about how nice it was to have a friend that she could do everything with.

She loved that she no longer felt lonely and that she now had someone to call when she wanted to have someone to play with.

Daffodil thought about how great it was that she would no longer feel like an outsider while everyone else played with their friends, and she sat by herself playing alone.

She smiled as she fell asleep and had a wonderful dream all night long.

The next morning, the two fairies woke up and made themselves a breakfast of berry pancakes and syrup.

Then, they went back outside to enjoy playing all morning again.

Again, they flew with the butterflies and the birds.

They played with the frogs and the turtles, and they picked berries fresh from the berry patch.

Then, they stopped by Elder Sage's house to thank her for introducing them.

"Glad to see you two are enjoying each other's company." Elder Sage smiled, offering them both a cup of berry tea.

"We are! We really are." the two fairies smiled, sipping their fresh berry tea.

From that day on, Daffodil and Daisy always had a best friend to go through life with.

The two fairies had many wonderful times, and they also had many challenging and sometimes sad times.

No matter what happened, though, they always knew that they had a wonderful best friend to go through life with.

They were by each other's side through everything, and knowing that they never had to go through life alone again meant that they would always have someone to count on.

This way, they were never the single fairy out anymore, but instead, they always had someone to enjoy life with.
Even as they grew and changed, they always had each other, and that is what made their friendship so beautiful.

Having good friends is an important part of life.

Making friends might be challenging, but once you make friends, it is important that you hold onto them.

Make sure that you always treat your friends nicely and that you always take care of your friends, and they will take care of you, too.

A good friend is hard to come by sometimes, but they last a lifetime, and they are incredibly special people to have in your life.

When you go through your life and start making wonderful friends, you can use these affirmations to help you stay true to your friends and enjoy better friendships:

"I am a great friend."
"I take care of my friends."
"I care about my friends."
"I am helpful to my friends."
"My friends are helpful to me."
"I appreciate my friends."
"I love my friends."
"I am grateful for my friends."
"I am grateful to be a friend."
"I appreciate being a friend."

Conclusion

Thank you so much for purchasing *Bedtime Meditation Short Stories for Kids*.

I hope that this book has helped you have many wonderful nights' sleep.

Remember: a good night's sleep is an important part of waking up feeling refreshed and ready to have a great day.

You should always practice doing everything you can to help you have a wonderful night's sleep every single night.

Meditation is not just for sleeping, either!

If you find yourself feeling overwhelmed, angry, stressed out, or even sad, you can always use the important meditation skills you learned right here in this book.

For example, next time you feel overwhelmed, try using the muscle relaxation practice you learned in this book.

Or, the next time you feel angry, try using a helpful breathing meditation.

These skills will help you in many ways in life, so be sure to keep practicing them!

Thank you again for purchasing *Bedtime Meditation Short Stories for Kids*.

If you really enjoyed this book and felt it helped you sleep better, be sure to let your parents know so they can leave a thoughtful review of how this book has helped you get better sleep each night.

That way, even more kids can have a great sleep!

CPSIA information can be obtained
at www.ICGtesting.com
Printed in the USA
LVHW030617250320
651144LV00009B/725